SECRETS

He spoke in a frantic whisper.

"I'd have gone for Mark and Simon, but they're helping with the meals. It's Kate. Nobody's seen her all day. I assumed she was in her office, meeting with parents. The phone was being answered earlier. But when I went up and knocked just now, there was no reply. I tried the door – it's locked – she never locks the office. I tried banging on the door. There was still no reply."

"Is there a spare key?" Mo asked.

Phil shook his head.

"I've never known her lock the door before."

"OK," said Mo, putting her arm lightly around Phil's waist. "Calm down. What do you want us to do?"

"There's only one thing we can do," Phil said, despairingly. "We have to force it open!"

MARK RUTHERFORD SCHOOL
ENGLISH DEPARTMENT

Other titles in the Point Crime series:

School for Terror
by Peter Beere

Formula for Murder
by Malcolm Rose

P●INT CRiME

DEADLY SECRETS

David Belbin

SCHOLASTIC INC.
New York Toronto London Auckland Sydney

If you purchased this book without a cover, you should be aware that this book is stolen property. It was reported as "unsold and destroyed" to the publisher, and neither the author nor the publisher has received any payment for this "stripped book."

No part of this publication may be reproduced in whole or in part, or stored in a retrieval system, or transmitted in any form or by any means, electronic, mechanical, photocopying, recording, or otherwise, without written permission of the publisher. For information regarding permission, write to Scholastic Children's Books, Scholastic Publications Ltd., 7–9 Pratt Street, London NW1 OAE, England.

ISBN 0-590-48318-8

Copyright © 1993 by David Belbin. All rights reserved. Published by Scholastic Inc., 555 Broadway, New York, NY 10012, by arrangement with Scholastic Children's Books, Scholastic Publications Ltd. POINT is a registered trademark of Scholastic Inc.

12 11 10 9 8 7 6 5 4 3 2 1   4 5 6 7 8 9/9

Printed in the U.S.A.   01

First Scholastic printing, June 1994

For Paul

DEADLY SECRETS

1

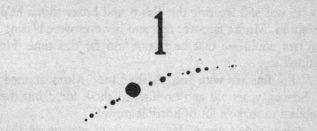

"I'm not going back!"

Adam stomped up the stairs to his bedroom. Slamming the door behind him, he picked up his guitar and plugged it into the amp. He cranked the bass and volume up to "maximum". Then he began to play, thrashing each chord like he was firing a machine gun. It took less than a minute for Mum to reach the top of the stairs and pound on the door.

"Adam! Stop that racket!"

Adam played one last chord and, without damping the strings, put the guitar down so that it was facing the front of the speaker. Mum banged on the door again.

"I've had it up to *here* with you, Adam Lane."

The hum from the speaker was beginning to build up, feeding back into the room as a wall of ugly, distorted sound.

"Adam!" Mum yelled.

As she opened the door, the noise broke, turning into a deafening, high-pitched whistle.

"That's it!"

Mum pulled the plug out of the wall socket and the guitar feedback died. Mum stood in front of Adam, who was still wearing the T-shirt and boxer shorts he'd slept in. Mum's face was red, and her eyes were blazing. Adam could see that he'd gone too far this time. He didn't care.

"I'm finished with you, Adam Lane," Mum shouted. "Sixteen years old and nothing to show for it but the ability to make a lot of horrible noise."

Adam didn't argue. He knew from experience that there was no point when she got like this.

"I've had enough, Adam. I've been there for you on my own for the last fourteen years. Now I want my life back. If you won't go back to school, retake your exams, fine. That's your choice. But you can find somewhere else to live. You can take your guitar with you, and your stereo and all your music and the things you call clothes, too. I'll give you a week."

This time it was Mum who slammed the door.

Adam sat down. She didn't mean it, of course. There was nowhere for Adam to go to. Give her five minutes, then he'd wander downstairs, make it up with her. Adam pulled on his one good pair of jeans and went into the bathroom for a wash. He threw soapy water at his face, then looked at himself in the mirror.

If he was on stage, with his band, he would look cool. His jeans were ripped just the right amount, within an inch of falling apart. His tie-dyed T-shirt clung tightly to his chest. Adam's long brown hair was curly and thick, covering his face. Adam didn't like his face much. His nose was too long. So was his chin. But, these days, it was fashionable for rock stars to be ugly.

Downstairs, another door slammed. Too late to make up with Mum. She was on a late at the supermarket. Time, Adam thought, for breakfast. It was half-past twelve. Adam found an unopened, A5 envelope propped up on the breakfast bar. On the back of it, Mum had printed in bright, red felt-tip: "I MEANT EVERY WORD!" Adam turned the envelope over. It was addressed to him. And he recognised the handwriting, too. He knew it from cards that came twice a year – once on his birthday, once at Christmas. But the author of the handwriting was a stranger: his father.

The letter was quite short.

> *Adam,*
> *Your mother wrote to me about your exam results. She says that she won't support you any more and now it's my turn. I don't know whether she really means it or not. However, you're at an age where you might be ready to leave home anyway. If that's the case, I've got a proposition for you.*

Adam read the letter with mounting disbelief. His parents had split up when he was two. He had rarely seen his father since. Simon Lane would show up for the occasional afternoon, always out of the blue. Twice, Adam had stayed with his father for a weekend, but the last time was when he was ten. Simon Lane was the Head of an English department in a secondary school, but, as far as Adam could tell, he had remarkably little ability to get on with children.

Adam thought that Simon was a bit like the TV character, Doctor Who – an eccentric man with no dress sense. His smile was sincere but permanently distracted. Like the Doctor, Simon Lane would show up every so often, whenever his Tardis happened to land him in the late twentieth century. On every visit he'd have a new image – leathers one time, grey suit another. He'd stick around for a while, then vanish, sometimes for years.

Now, it seemed, Simon Lane had a new job at a small, private school in Yorkshire. "*I know that you don't want to go back to school,*" Adam's father wrote, "*but this one is different. Maybe you'd enjoy it. Maybe we could get to know each other a little before it's too late.*"

He had enclosed a brochure for the place, "Beechwood Grange Free School". The name was vaguely familiar to Adam, but he couldn't recall where he'd heard it. According to the brochure, Beechwood wasn't just for rich kids. "Fees are agreed according to the family's ability to pay. You can't put a value on education. We ask everyone to give as much as they can afford." That sounded fair enough to Adam, although calling it a "free" school was a bit much. Presumably, Dad could get him in at a specially reduced rate.

The brochure showed a beautiful old building, surrounded by lush greenery. At the bottom of the last page was a list of "distinguished alumni". Their names meant nothing to Adam: "Sandy Appleton, actor; Elijah Merry, architect; Antonia Gaughan, philosopher;

Robert Joyce, industrialist; Suzanne Windley, film director; Paul Nelson, musician."

Paul Nelson: Adam did a double take. Not *the* Paul Nelson, the guy who founded Call to Arms, the best heavy metal group of the early eighties? Who else could it be? Admittedly, Nelson had mellowed out since then – his records sounded more like Phil Collins than Metallica, but his old stuff was sampled and stolen from all the time. That would be something to tell the old members of his band, who had chucked music to concentrate on their GCSEs. "I'm going to the same school as Paul Nelson." That would show them.

When she got home, Adam's mum tried her hardest to make Adam change his mind. She kept quoting bits of the brochure to him and laughing.

" 'Founded in 1967' – you know what that means – run by a load of hippies whose idea of education was taking LSD and *finding themselves*. Look at this: 'dedicated teachers encourage freedom of expression and personal growth' – in other words, they let you do what you like! And this: 'We have no rules and no set curriculum. Students run their own lives and decide their own individual programme of study'." She sighed. "Adam, you can't go there! It's a skiver's paradise, a place where rich people send the kids they can't control! You know, I've got a feeling I read about that school in the paper not so long ago. There was some kind of a scandal. . . ."

Adam interrupted. "You're scraping the barrel, Mum. Stop it."

Adam didn't understand adults: one minute Mum was

throwing him out, the next she was crying because he wanted to move two hundred miles away. Mum even said that she'd try to get him a job in the warehouse of the supermarket which she managed, if that was what he wanted. But it was too late. Adam was going back to school. Mum's last words on the subject were, "Ask your dad why he's working there. The pay'll be lousy and he never had any time for trendy ideas before. It wouldn't surprise me if he's been sacked and that's the only place that will have him."

But Adam didn't ask Simon Lane any questions when they met. He didn't feel that he knew his father well enough. Mum was at work when Dad came to collect him. Simon Lane was driving a rusty Escort, and wearing trainers, a sweatshirt and jeans. Mr Casual. He greeted Adam warmly. After that, though, they were awkward with each other. To make matters worse, there wasn't room in the car for Adam's guitar and amplifier. Dad had several suitcases and boxes in the car already.

"Is that all you're taking?" Adam asked. "I'd have thought you'd have a lorry load of stuff to move."

Dad shook his head. "I sold the furniture with the flat. I threw a lot away, gave some stuff to Oxfam. I want to make a fresh start. Possessions get in the way."

The journey lasted four hours. Adam and his father made small talk at first, but soon lapsed into silence. They came off the motorway near Huddersfield.

"By the way," Dad said, "I suppose you've heard some gossip about the Grange School?"

Adam shook his head.

"Nothing."

"I doubt that. But, whatever you've heard, it's not like that any more."

"I told you," Adam insisted, "I hadn't heard of the place until last week. Is there something I should know?"

Dad didn't reply. Maybe it was because he was concentrating on driving. The road had become narrower and it was starting to rain. When Adam's father spoke again, it was on a different subject.

"At this school everyone's on a first-name basis. The kids won't call me 'Sir', or 'Mr Lane'. They'll call me Simon."

"So?"

"So I thought it might be a good idea if you called me Simon, too."

Adam looked at his father's lined face. Simon Lane's dark eyes stared unblinking at the road ahead. His greasy hair was thinning at the top but had started to grow long at the sides. This first-name thing, Adam decided, was another example of his father trying to change his image. Simon had a new job in an experimental "free" school, so he was turning into a trendy teacher, who treated his son just the same as the other kids. Some chance.

"We could see it as a new start," his father said, after a while. "It's time we got to know each other properly, as adults. What do you say?"

Adam was forced to reply this time. He took a deep breath.

"OK," he said, trying to sound like none of this mattered very much. "If that's what you want, *Simon*."

* * *

They drove past signs for places with names that seemed to come from the middle ages: Halifax, Mytholmroyd, Hebblethwaite, Hebden Bridge. One of the larger signs listed Bradford as being twenty miles away – a city, which would have films and concerts. But the place Adam was going to sat in the middle of nowhere. Bradford might as well be London, the city Adam had just left.

"This is it."

They turned down a narrow lane. Adam had expected to find grand gates, a sign at least, but all he could see were the words "Grange School" crudely painted onto a dry-stone wall.

"Watch yourself now," Dad said. "This may be a little bumpy."

He wasn't exaggerating. The steep road was not tarmacked. Grass grew down the middle and there were numerous pot-holes and loose stones. If another vehicle were to come towards them, there was no room for it to pass. One car would have to reverse all the way back.

"This isn't like the photo," Adam said. "This is grotty."

"Wait 'til we turn the corner."

Simon sounded the car's horn as they took a tight bend. Ahead of them, through the drizzle, were the beech woods shown in the brochure. A narrow bridge stretched across a river.

"You'll see the Grange in a moment," Dad said.

Suddenly, there was a sharp cracking noise.

"What the. . . ?"

Simon hit the brakes and the Escort skidded into the

dry-stone wall on their right. Adam looked at the crack in the driver's door window. Then he saw something beyond it.

"Duck!"

The second blast shattered the window completely. Simon swore, loudly. Adam stared through the missing window. Then he opened the passenger door.

"Stay down!"

"No."

A cold, wet wind blew onto Adam's face. He thought that he had made out a figure in a green coat, disappearing into the woodland. But now he could see nothing. He got back into the car. Dad was brushing off the shards of glass which covered his sweatshirt. He held up a shotgun pellet.

"Couldn't have hurt us at that distance," Dad said. "Probably a farmer shooting at a rabbit."

Adam said nothing. In the distance, he thought that he heard someone laughing.

2

"It wouldn't have been one of ours," Kate Dance told Adam and Simon as they sat in her study's uncomfortable armchairs. "We only have one student here today. The rest don't arrive until Monday. And anyway, every year, the school council votes not to allow the possession of any kind of weapons, even knives. . . ."

"Hold on," said Adam. "I thought this place didn't have any rules?"

"*This place*," said Ms Dance, frostily, "doesn't have any *teacher-imposed* rules. However, each year the whole body of students agree certain *guidelines* which will ensure the smooth running of the school."

"You mean that there's a vote?"

"Usually, there's no need for a vote. Decisions are arrived at by consensus."

Behind her antique desk, Ms Dance swivelled her

leather-backed chair so that she faced away from Adam. She began talking to Simon about his timetable: boring stuff about which students were doing which courses and which ones were "improvising". Adam took this to mean that they were doing as they pleased. Lessons were divided into one-to-one "tutorials" and small group "sessions". Adam found himself gazing at Kate Dance. She looked like a Headteacher: stern and sexless. He could see that she had once been a beautiful woman. But now her greying hair was close cropped and this, together with her metal-rimmed glasses, made her high-cheek-boned face look severe. She wore a grey linen suit, rather than the casual clothes Adam would have expected at a "free" school. Kate seemed to sense Adam staring at her. She turned to face him.

"Simon and I will be quite a while," she said. "We don't want you getting bored."

Adam shrugged. Was this a dig? Had she been reading his old reports, many of which included the phrase "easily bored"?

"Why don't you check the place out?" Simon suggested.

What Adam really wanted was a mug of coffee. They hadn't been offered anything since they arrived. But it looked like he'd have to find one on his own.

"OK," Adam said. "I'm going."

The Grange was a large, square, eighteenth-century building with cold, high-ceilinged rooms. The Head and Deputy lived on the first floor. The students lived in dormitories in the grounds, a short walk away.

For a few minutes Adam wandered aimlessly from room to room, each one deserted. The place had the feel of a stately home gone to seed. Already, it bored him. By the time Adam got to the library, he realised that he couldn't remember the way back to the Head's study.

"Where is everybody?" he asked aloud.

"They're on holiday," a female voice answered from somewhere beyond the stacks of books. "Term doesn't start for two days."

Adam was taken aback. He walked around, but couldn't see anyone.

"Where are you?"

No reply. At the other end of the library there were no books. The wall was lined with study cubicles. In front of these were several tables with easy chairs around them. A large window overlooked the river. Adam kept looking for the girl who'd spoken to him. He was embarrassed. It wasn't as though he was in the habit of talking to himself. Suddenly, a voice spoke from behind him. "You must be Adam Lane."

Adam turned around. The voice was girlish but its owner was a woman: twenty, at least. She was tall, with a full figure. Her pale face might have seemed beautiful, were it not for the way her auburn hair was cut close, like the Head's.

"How do you know my name?" Adam asked.

"My aunt's Kate Dance, the Headteacher. That's why I'm allowed here out of term time. There's a strict rule that students don't stay in the holidays. Otherwise, some of them would never leave."

"They like it that much, huh?"

"Some. Others just hate home a lot more."

Adam laughed, though he wasn't sure that she'd

meant to make a joke. She had one of those deliberately girly voices, he decided, the kind that had a sarcastic edge to it. With people like that, you could never tell whether they were mocking you or not.

"You're a student here?" he asked, politely.

"I'm in the Upper Sixth. I take 'A' levels next year."

"They call it year 13 now."

"I don't think so," the girl said. "I'm superstitious, you see."

This time Adam didn't laugh, but the girl did.

"I'm Naomi," she said when she'd finished, in a voice sweeter than before. Then she offered him her hand to shake. "Would you like me to show you the grounds?"

"All right," he said, surprised to find how cool her fingers were. "Thanks."

Outside, it had stopped raining. Naomi pointed to two large stone barns on the edge of the river.

"Those are the dormitories."

"Which one do you live in?"

She pointed to the smaller one.

"Are they mixed?"

Naomi giggled.

"They were once, but it caused some problems. The boys have the bigger dorm. There are less girls than boys, I'm afraid."

"How many pupils . . . I mean students, are there altogether?"

"Just under fifty. Numbers are down at the moment. Here, this is the new teaching block. It's only been up a year."

The new block was built of brick. It had the same

square shape as the Grange itself, but was much smaller, with large windows.

"Only half of it is being used at the moment," Naomi told him. "The language and science labs. Kate's hoping to get TV and music recording studios equipped, when she can raise the money."

They came to the river. Across it were the dense beech woods which gave the school its name. From where they were standing, the woods looked mysterious, and a little threatening.

"Hi!"

Simon and Kate were walking down the path from the Grange. Adam waved.

"Oh," said Naomi. "I forgot to show you where the other teachers live."

They followed the adults to a small cottage out of sight of the dormitories.

"All of them live *there*?" Adam asked.

He could see why his father had needed to get rid of most of his possessions.

"No," Naomi replied. "Four teachers live in the village, the ones who've been here a long time. There's just Mark and your dad living there this term. Oh, and Mo, when she's around."

"Mo?"

"Mo Highton, the school counsellor."

"We didn't have those in Ealing."

"You're lucky," Naomi said, with feeling. "She's just a busy-body, if you ask me."

She smiled at Adam. As they walked up the cottage path, a little sun broke through the dingy clouds. This isn't such a bad place, he thought.

They joined the two teachers in the cottage's kitchen. Kate Dance was smiling.

"I'm glad you two found each other," she said. "I hope you're going to be great friends."

"I'm sure we are," Naomi smiled back.

"Come on, Adam," his father told him. "It's time we moved our stuff in out of the car."

"Yes," said Kate, "and you'd better get back to your studies, young lady. You've got a lot of catching up to do."

Naomi grinned, then followed Kate back to the Grange.

"See you later."

Naomi was all right, Adam decided. He was pleased that she wasn't a swot, as he'd feared when he saw her in the library. Maybe they would get along.

He and Simon drove up to the dormitory, unlocked it, and dumped Adam's stuff in the foyer. Then they carried Simon's things up to the cottage, which wasn't accessible by car. By the time they'd finished, Adam was exhausted. All he wanted to do was lie down. But first he had to find a room to do it in.

The boys' dormitories contained twenty identical rooms, each with bunk beds. None of them were locked – they didn't appear to have locks – but all showed signs of occupation. Adam had hoped to find a room to himself, but it seemed he had no chance. Finally, he decided to settle for the end room. It was no different from the others, but it had a good view, and the window opened fully, unlike some of the others. Also, he guessed that he was less likely to be disturbed by other boys traipsing in and out.

As he carried his belongings into the room, Adam tried to imagine what the other occupant was like. He had a Black Sabbath poster next to the bed, and there was a torn leather jacket on the bottom bunk, so Adam guessed he'd better take the top one. There were no clothes in the wardrobe, but there was a Theakston's bitter ashtray, which hadn't been washed out. The wardrobe backed straight onto the wall. Adam noticed that the stone at the bottom was loose. He pulled it out and felt around. Nothing. Thirsty, Adam turned on the cold tap by the small sink, cupped his hands, and drank ice-cold water until he'd had his fill. It tasted brilliant – hard and sweet, better than anything he'd had from a bottle. Then he got onto the top bunk and, despite the flabby mattress, fell immediately into a deep, dreamless sleep.

He woke to a loud creaking sound, then a banging. It took Adam a few moments to remember where he was. Uneasily, he turned over to see what was going on. A tall, long-haired figure in a green kagoul stared back at him with angry eyes.

"You're dead," he said.

3

Adam flinched, and said nothing. The tall boy brushed the thick fringe away from his large eyes, then let out a torrent of obscenities, ending with:

". . . what do you think you're doing in my room?"

Awake now, Adam decided to brazen it out.

"Actually," he said, "I was about to ask you the same thing. No-one's supposed to be here until the day after tomorrow."

"Then you shouldn't be, either."

"My father works here."

Adam got down from his bunk and onto the floor. If they were going to fight, he wanted to be standing up. Adam was six feet tall. The other boy was at least two inches taller and a stone heavier.

"Look," said Adam, "I didn't know that this was

your room. I chose it because it was the end one. Really, I'd prefer one by myself."

His opponent seemed to relax a little. The threat of violence seemed to be over.

"I'm Adam Lane."

Awkwardly, Adam held out his hand for the other boy to shake, but was ignored. Instead, the room's owner pulled a packet of Winstons from the pocket of his kagoul and lit one, without offering the pack to Adam.

"I'm Forrest," he said.

"Just 'Forrest'?"

"Yes."

"Don't the students here use first names?"

"They do," said Forrest, as though Adam had asked a stupid question. "That's why I never use mine."

Adam picked up one of his bags.

"I'll find another room, then."

Forrest blew smoke towards Adam's face. "Tell anyone you saw me and I'll have you. Got that?"

"If you say so."

Forrest blew more smoke at him. Adam wanted to get away from him as quickly as possible.

"If you want a room to yourself, take number eleven. Steven Crosby isn't coming back."

"How do you know?"

"Because I told him what would happen to him if he did."

Room eleven had no river view and the window barely opened at all. The bottom mattress was useless, so Adam decided to sleep on top. Maybe he'd move them round later. Yellow paint flaked from the room's walls. It would do, Adam supposed, contemplating the low ceiling directly above him. There was no way that he could share a room with someone like Forrest.

"Adam?"

It was Naomi's voice. Adam pulled himself down from the bunk and examined himself in the mirror above the sink. He looked a mess. His jeans were new and offensively clean. His T-shirt, on the other hand, looked like he'd slept in it for a week, which he had. His hair was filthy and over-long, making his face look narrow. He checked his watch. It was six.

"Adam? Are you in here?"

Adam pushed his hair behind his neck and went to the door. Naomi stood in the corridor with a steaming mug of coffee in her hand.

"Sorry," Adam said. "I was asleep."

"Simon said that you take one sugar. I hope that's right."

Adam nodded.

"We're having dinner at the Grange in half an hour. You should make the most of it. Kate's a good cook. But after tomorrow you'll eat in dorm."

"In dorm?"

"That's right. We all cook for each other. Can you cook?"

"Are you kidding?"

Naomi grinned. "You'll learn, I guess. The girls' food is dreadful, so who knows what the boys' is like."

Adam sipped the hot coffee. Naomi beamed at him.

"I've put the water-heater on," she said, as she turned to go, "if you'd like a shower before we eat."

"Yes," said Adam. "Good idea."

He undressed, got out his wash bag and a towel, then found the bathroom. The shower seemed to have just three positions: red hot, tepid and freezing. Adam settled for luke-warm and got out of it as quickly as possible. He realised that he would have to go to dinner with wet hair. There was no Mum to borrow a hair-drier from. Leaving the bathroom, he glanced down the unlit corridor. Forrest's door remained closed.

Adam went back to room eleven and threw his wet towel onto the bottom bunk. Only then did he realise that he was not alone.

"You've got good taste."

Forrest lay on the floor of Adam's room. He had opened one of Adam's bags. CDs were scattered everywhere. Forrest's eyes had that same mocking look which Adam had first seen in Naomi earlier. He held up Adam's copy of *Dirty* by Sonic Youth.

"I haven't heard this yet. Can I borrow it?"

It was clear that Adam didn't have much choice.

Forrest got up slowly. There was something threatening about his every movement – a threat reinforced by the half smile on his face.

"You'd better get a move on," he said, as he opened Adam's door. "You don't want to be late for dinner."

The dining room in the Grange was impressively old fashioned. The portraits on the walls had elaborate frames. The table was long and heavy, with a silver service meticulously set out at one end of it. A wood fire burnt in the grate. But Adam's eyes didn't linger on any of these details. He was more taken by Naomi. She wore a floral summer dress which hugged her figure. With a little make-up on she looked twenty-five, at least. It isn't fair, Adam thought, that girls can look so much older. Boys his age didn't have a chance.

Kate carried in two large dishes of lasagne, one of them vegetarian, while Simon poured red wine for everyone. Two places, Adam noticed, were empty.

"Mark and Mo will be along shortly," Kate told the other three. "She's probably having to drag him away from his typewriter. We'll start without them."

Ravenous, Adam and his father tore into the pasta, while Kate and Naomi ate their smaller portions in silence. Adam had nearly finished his helping when the other diners arrived. They were a man and a woman, both in their twenties.

"Sorry we're late," the woman said, in a Yorkshire accent.

She had long mousy hair which curled unevenly. She wore an arran sweater with a short, brown, corduroy skirt. The man behind her also had curly hair, but it was thick and golden with a centre parting and locks that partially obscured his face. He was in his early twenties, Adam guessed. She was nearer thirty.

"Come in," Kate welcomed them. "You've both met Simon. This is his son, Adam. Adam, this is Mark Rhodes and Mo Highton. They live in the cottage with your father."

Adam said hello. The couple sat down and helped themselves to food. Then Adam and his father had a second helping. Mo Highton ate hungrily, but Mark Rhodes seemed more interested in talking to Simon. They were talking about English teaching, a topic which sent Adam to sleep. At least that was one subject which he didn't have to take again.

"Shakespeare," Mark Rhodes was arguing, "is overrated. He's an authoritarian tool – the heart of the dead white male establishment. The reason the government insists on him being taught to fourteen-year-olds is that he puts students to sleep."

"Certainly had that effect on me," Adam muttered.

Naomi whispered conspiratorially. "He's trying to impress his new boss."

Simon was trying to put Mark in his place.

"We can't deny our students Shakespeare because he's often taught badly. We have to have a balance of approaches. Naomi here, for instance, has to tackle *Hamlet* and *Othello* for her 'A' level exam."

"Worse luck," Naomi said.

"If you're so keen on the classics," Mark forced home his point, "why did you quit your job in Coventry for one that pays half the salary?"

This was the question Adam wanted to know the answer to. But before Simon could reply, Kate interrupted. "Simon's had a long drive today. I'm sure he's tired. Why don't you save the discussion for another day? I'm afraid that I still have some work to do. Naomi, will you sort out the coffee and do the dishes?"

Naomi nodded. Kate stood. Mo stood up, too.

"Can I have a quick word, Kate, in private?"

The two women left together.

Adam was in no hurry to leave. The dorm had a TV and video room, but he didn't want to encounter Forrest there. He offered to help Naomi wash the dishes. As he carried crockery down the corridor to the kitchen, Adam could hear voices echoing from the Head's study. The higher one was Mo Highton's.

"If I'm right, it's been going on all summer!"

Kate's reply was calmer.

"But you're only guessing, Mo. Do you think that I don't know what goes on in my own school?"

"We can't afford something like that happening again."

Kate's voice rose.

"You're exaggerating, as usual."

Mo sounded aggrieved.

"You think that *I'm* exaggerating. How do you think it would look in the newspapers?"

Kate's voice became fiercer.

"That sounds dangerously like a threat to me. Watch your step, Mo. And don't mention what you've told me to anyone else. I'll look into it. Meanwhile, remember, we still don't know who . . ."

"Come on."

Naomi stood behind Adam, looking irritated. Adam had blocked the corridor in order to hear the conversation. He was embarrassed and moved away quickly.

"It's not as interesting as it sounds," Naomi told him in the kitchen. They put the dishes in soak and put the coffee-maker on.

"Do you know what they're talking about?" Adam asked Naomi.

She shook her head.

"Kate and I aren't that close," she said. "Tell me about Simon. Why did he pack in his old job and come to work here?"

"No idea," Adam told her. "I hardly know him, to be honest. I'm not even sure if I like him. Does that sound awful to you?"

"No," Naomi said, squeezing his arm. "It sounds like we've got an awful lot in common."

Naomi insisted on Adam wearing an apron over his shabby clothes. As he fumbled with putting it on, she took the straps and tied them for him, behind his back. Her every touch made Adam tingle with excitement.

Adam had never had a girlfriend. Music always seemed more important. But he didn't have a band any more. He hadn't even brought his guitar with him. Now there was time for the other stuff – romance, or sex, call it what you like. It had always made him nervous before, except when he was putting his feelings into a song.

"Last day of freedom tomorrow," Naomi told him, "before classes begin. How'd you like to go for a walk with me? I could show you the countryside around the school."

"Sounds great," Adam told her.

He tried to make the dishwashing, and the conversation, last as long as he could. Soon, however, the coffee was ready, the dishes done. Naomi carried the pot through, then took a cup to Kate. She didn't return. Mo had already left. Mark and Simon drank their coffee quickly, then elected to go back to the teachers' cottage. Adam had no choice but to return to the lonely dormitory. He hoped that Naomi would show up, and Forrest wouldn't.

4

Adam saw nobody for the rest of his first evening at the Grange, and went to bed early. In the morning, he put on a new pair of jeans and clean T-shirt, anticipating Naomi's arrival. She didn't come until ten. In her dufflecoat and Timberland boots she looked once more like a schoolgirl, not a woman beyond his grasp. Adam felt an optimistic buzz as they set off, side by side.

Sun blazed down on the Pennine countryside. Naomi led Adam along a narrow path to Throstleroyd Crags.

"This might be the last proper day of summer," she said. "We ought to make the most of it."

"What have you done all summer?" Adam asked, as they left the woodland and the path led them onto open fields.

"I stayed at the Grange. I read a bit, watched videos,

the usual. Kate and Mark occasionally found time to help me with school work. I missed quite a bit of time through illness last year, so I've got a lot of catching up to do."

"Illness?"

"Nothing serious," Naomi said, evasively.

It must be a woman's thing, Adam thought, and changed the subject.

"Why's Mark stayed here over the summer? Don't the teachers go away?"

"All except for Aunt Kate, yes. Mark did go away for a few days. But he's writing a novel. He wanted to stay in the school cottage because it's so quiet in the holidays – he can get lots of work done."

Adam watched as a red grouse flew low over the crags ahead.

"What about you? Why didn't you go away with your parents?"

Naomi looked away from him. At first he thought that she, too, was looking at the grouse. But then she spoke, and he realised that she didn't want him to see the expression on her face.

"My mother died when I was young. She never married my father. He's not very interested in me. He travels a lot. I joined him for a week in July, but it was work, work, work, so I came back here to Aunt Kate."

"What does your father do?"

Naomi shrugged.

"Not much. He's quite rich, I suppose."

It occurred to Adam that Naomi's father was probably subsidising his, Adam's, education. He decided to change the subject.

"Do you get on well with Kate?"

"Most of the time," Naomi said. "It's not as if I have much choice. Sometimes she's very kind to me. She reminds me of my mum. Other times she can be a bit of a tyrant. It goes with the job, I suppose."

They were at the rocks now, and Adam was glad that he was wearing his heavy shoes. They clambered over the crags and down to the river. The climb was steep and they picked up speed as they descended. Once they were off the rocks both of them were running. They had so much momentum that it was impossible to stop. Adam found himself skidding on the damp grass, heading straight into the river.

"Grab me!"

Naomi threw herself at Adam and, intertwined, they fell to the ground, stopping a few feet short of the river's edge. They lay there, a bundle of grass-stained blue jeans, laughing. Slowly, they disentangled themselves. Adam stood. He tried to help Naomi up, too. She shook him off.

"Never do anything for a girl at Beechwood unless she asks you to," Naomi lectured him. "We're not the weaker sex here."

"I never . . ."

Adam stopped. The mood of a moment ago had totally gone. He didn't know what had got into Naomi. He looked back over the valley, to the woods which hid the Grange school. On the hill overlooking the woods stood someone in a green kagoul.

"Do you know who that is?" he asked, pointing out the green figure to Naomi. She shook her head.

"You get lots of walkers round here."

Adam didn't think it was just another walker. He told Naomi about Forrest.

"What was he doing in school?" she said.

"How should I know? But I reckon he's the one who shot at Simon and me."

Naomi shook her head.

"What motive would he have?"

Adam shrugged. They started to walk upriver, in the opposite direction from the Grange.

"Shouldn't we be getting back?" Adam asked.

"Tired?"

"Only a little."

"Well, I'm worn out. Come on. We're only a mile from Hebblethwaite. We can get a lift back from there."

Naomi set a strong pace along the river bank. Then they took a left turn through a field full of cotton grass, before climbing a steep, grassy hill. When they were at the top, the village lay in front of them. It was a warren of grey terraced houses with a small square and a church in the middle. There was one street of shops, with a pub at each end.

"Been here before?" Naomi asked.

"No."

"Why don't you have a quick look around? I've got some business to do. Meet you in the square in a few minutes."

She darted off into the village. Adam ambled towards the shopping street. He didn't suppose the shops would be any good. He was right. There was no record shop. The book shop was mainly aimed at ramblers and climbers. Then there was a Co-op, a butcher's, a greengrocer's and a sweet shop. That was it. Anyone driving through might call the village picturesque, but Adam wouldn't be coming back in a hurry.

He sat in the square on a bench by the phone box, wondering what was keeping Naomi occupied. Then he heard a shrill hooting.

"Over here!"

Naomi was behind the wheel of a green 2CV.

"Get in."

Adam opened the passenger door.

"Is this *yours*?"

"No, it's Kate's. She's been having it serviced. I said I'd pick it up for her. What did you think of the village?"

Adam told her. Inwardly, he was disappointed. He'd thought that the purpose of the walk was for Naomi to be with him, not to run an errand for her aunt.

"You want a record shop? There's a little one in Hebden Bridge. That's only half an hour from here."

"It's not like I'm desperate. I've only been here for a day."

Naomi shook her head.

"I'd been meaning to do some shopping there myself. And it's not often I get to use the car."

They drove off. Naomi drove fast and near the centre of the road. A nasty thought occurred to Adam.

"Have you got a . . . driving licence?"

Naomi flashed a wicked grin at him.

"You think Kate doesn't believe in rules so she'd let me drive a car without insurance or a licence?"

"Well . . ."

"Forget it. Kate's got a saying: 'to live outside the law

you must be honest'. She won't let anyone connected with the school do anything remotely illegal. She doesn't want the school's reputation damaged."

"When did you pass your test?"

"A while back."

The record shop was great: full of obscure singles and bootlegs much cheaper than you'd find them in London. Most of the music wasn't to Adam's taste, but he found a live Pixies CD of the tour where they supported U2, and snapped it up. When Naomi returned half an hour later, he was in a much perkier mood. She put down her Boots carrier bag and flicked aimlessly through the racks of old albums.

"What sort of music do you like?" Adam wanted to know.

"Classical, mainly."

He hated people who said that. It removed all possibility of conversation. He reached into the pile she was looking through. There was a recent solo album by Paul Nelson.

"Didn't he used to go to Grange School?" he asked Naomi.

Naomi didn't reply. Adam went on. "He used to be in a band called Call to Arms. They were big in the early eighties. I thought the brochure said . . ."

"Aye, he used to go to school near here," the man behind the counter interrupted. "He comes back now and then, too. Came in here once – spent nearly fifty quid – all sorts of different stuff he bought: rap, metal, roots music . . ."

"Can't say I like his stuff any more," Adam said,

pleased to strike up the conversation. "Too middle of the road."

"I'm with you there," said the shop's owner. "But the three albums he made with Call to Arms, they were classics, every one of them."

"Did you ever see them play?" Adam started to ask, but Naomi was impatient.

"Come on, Adam," she said, brusquely. "We'll be late for dinner."

"Sorry," he said, when they were in the car. "You were getting bored."

"I didn't mean to snap at you," Naomi replied, in her former, cheerful tone. "I get like that sometimes. Don't take it personally."

Back at school, the pre-term staff meeting had just ended. They passed several teachers returning to the village. Adam saw that the window on Simon's Escort had been fixed, though you could still see marks where shotgun pellets had damaged the bodywork.

There were the same people for dinner as the previous night, with one addition. Phil Merchant, the Deputy Head, was a thin man, who wore pressed trousers and a nylon shirt. He looked like he'd be more comfortable in a suit. His hair was very short, but he had long sideburns which looked silly. He asked Mark Rhodes about the book that he was writing.

"What's the subject, again?"

Mark put down the chicken bone which he'd been picking at.

"The tyranny of the mediocre," he said, "and the

terrorism of the mundane. I see myself as part of the 'dirty realism' school."

Merchant looked bemused.

"Yes, but . . . what's the plot?" he asked.

Rhodes gave Merchant a look which suggested he thought that the older man was a philistine.

"Plot is a bourgeois concept which I try to avoid," he replied, tersely. "You can keep it for detective novels."

This comment killed the conversation. As soon as everyone had finished eating, Mark volunteered to help Naomi wash up. Phil Merchant asked Adam a few questions about his studies, and how he'd found the school so far.

"It's different," Adam said, tactfully.

"You'll meet a lot of interesting people here, from all sorts of different backgrounds and cultures. You can learn a lot from them. Of course, we have our share of unsavoury types too, but if you're wise, you'll stay out of their way. . . ."

Adam wondered if he was referring to Forrest. Soon, Merchant left. Mo went off with Kate. Maybe they were going to continue their argument of the previous night. Adam was left alone with Simon, for the first time since they'd arrived.

"How's the dorm?" Simon asked.

"Not bad. It'll be better when there are more people around."

"Want to come up to the cottage tonight, watch some TV with me?"

Adam shook his head. He didn't want to hang around with teachers, even if they were his father. Also, he was hoping that Naomi might visit him. Simon guessed what was on his mind.

"You're getting on well with Kate's niece, aren't you?"

"She's all right."

"Don't get too interested," Simon warned him, gently. "She's a bit out of your league, mate."

"I know."

"Good."

Back in the dorm, Adam thought about what Simon had said. The conversation about Naomi was the nearest they'd ever had to a man-to-man talk. But he would have rather the subject had been different. He already liked her too much.

There was music coming from Forrest's room. It was a Nirvana album called *Hormoning*, an expensive Japanese import. Adam was impressed that Forrest owned it. He'd had to save up for a month before buying his own copy.

Hours later, Adam was getting into bed, disappointed that Naomi hadn't appeared. He could still hear Nirvana. It occurred to Adam to check his own collection. It was as he'd feared. The Nirvana CD, along with several others, was missing. Adam swore aloud. There was only one thing to do: confront Forrest now. Adam got dressed again and hurried down the corridor. He had to see Forrest before he got nervous and bottled it.

Adam banged loudly on Forrest's door. There was no reply. Bracing himself, Adam went in. The window of Forrest's room was open. He had left his CD player on, programmed to continuous random play. Adam ejected the disc. From the window, he heard an owl and the soft rush of the river. Then he heard a distinct thud in the distance, like the sound of a gun being fired. Maybe Forrest was out shooting at cars.

There were silver discs scattered across the floor. Adam took the ones that belonged to him, put them in their cases, and returned to his room. Adam would be glad when tomorrow came and he was no longer alone in the building with Forrest. He listened out carefully for the bully's return, but all he heard was the wind and the rain.

5

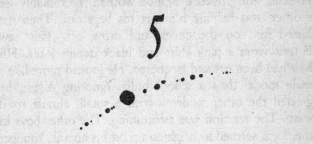

All day the students arrived. Teachers took turns on traffic duty, making sure that cars didn't collide on the narrow lane down to the school. However, some parents, particularly those of new students, insisted on driving down to the Grange itself. Phil Merchant treated each one with oily charm and despatched them as quickly as possible.

"Where's Kate?" Adam asked Naomi. "I'd have thought she'd be here to meet people."

"Her office door is closed," Naomi told him. "Which means she doesn't want to be disturbed – I guess she's talking to parents."

Simon was in charge of sorting out accommodation in the boys' dorm.

"You're sharing with someone called Steven Crosby," he told Adam. "He hasn't shown up yet."

And he won't show up, either, Adam thought – not if Forrest had his way with him.

Forrest was one of the last to arrive. At first, Adam didn't recognise the lad. All he saw was a glamorous-looking boy getting out of a new registration red Porsche. An attractive blonde woman, presumably his mother, was helping him get his bags out. Then she kissed him on the cheek and drove off. This new Forrest wore a pink shirt and black denim jeans. His hair had been cut and lacquered. He looked more like a male model than a school bully. Ignoring Adam, he greeted the other students with a small, almost royal wave. The reaction was astonishing. The other boys in the dorm seemed to brighten up on his arrival. Younger boys rushed to carry in his bags. Everyone asked about his holiday.

"The usual thing – San Tropez, San Francisco, Malibu. I managed to spend a week alone on retreat in Scotland . . ." As he said this he raised his eyes and, just for a moment, his glance met Adam's. "That was the best part," he went on, "living rough, pitching my tent where I felt like it, talking to whatever locals I ran into. . . ."

It was impossible to mistake the admiring glances. Forrest was really popular. There was no question of him asking the others about their holidays, either. He was the centre of attention, and happy to keep it that way.

"Could I interrupt for a moment?"

Phil Merchant had come in without anyone noticing. "I've just come to remind you that there's a meeting for new students in the Grange in five minutes. Also, that the rest of you ought to have sorted out a cooking rota.

If dinner's going to be on time, you'll need to start soon."

A number of boys got up to go to the meeting. Adam supposed he'd better join them. It was unlikely that he'd learn anything, but he might make some new friends. This last notion quickly disappeared when he got into the Grange. Most of the eleven new kids were twelve or thirteen. There was one scholarly-looking boy nearer Adam's age, with owlish glasses and an incredibly thin frame. Adam couldn't see himself getting on with him. And there was a fat, blonde girl, who Adam took to be fourteen or fifteen. She latched onto Adam immediately.

"My name's Tanya. What's yours? Why'd you come here? My parents read about this place in the newspaper. Before that they'd given up on finding a school that would take me."

Adam felt compelled to ask.

"Why?"

Tanya replied.

"I set fire to things."

"Oh."

"Hello, everybody."

Phil Merchant stood at the front of the small hall.

"On behalf of Kate Dance and the rest of the staff, I'd like to welcome you to Beechwood Grange School. I'm Mr Merchant, and my first name's Phil. Call me whichever you feel most comfortable with. But please don't call me 'Sir', even though you might mean it as a mark of respect. Everybody's equal here. We expect to learn as much from you as you do from us."

"You might learn more than you bargained for," Tanya muttered.

Phil ran through a list of administrative details to do with laundry, timetables and eating arrangements.

"I'm sorry that the Head can't be with you this evening," Phil went on. "You'll meet her at assembly tomorrow. But before you go off to dinner, I would like to introduce you to another very important person – Mo Highton, our school counsellor."

Mo smiled at Phil, who immediately left the hall. Then she came and sat on the platform where Phil had been standing.

"I'm not a teacher," she announced. "I used to be one, but I found that what I really enjoyed was working with students on a one-to-one basis. Therefore I'm glad to be here, where most of the teaching is done that way. I hope that you'll like it here, too."

Adam found himself warming to Mo. The counsellor hadn't made much impression on him at dinner on the previous two nights. Now he found her voice gentle, relaxing.

"However, like any new school, this can be a confusing and frightening place. And, of course, the Grange isn't like just any old school. There are a lot of freedoms for you to get used to. No-one makes you attend sessions, for instance. No-one tells you when to go to bed at night. You can even smoke cigarettes, if that's what you want, though you can expect to be reminded of all the horrible diseases that smoking causes."

There were a couple of sniggers at this. Mo uncrossed her legs and carried on.

"At first, I'm sure, you'll want to make the most of these freedoms. The last thing you'll want is some fuddy-duddy like me warning you that they come with a price. But, remember – with freedom comes responsibility, and not everyone is as responsible as they should be . . ."

Mo continued to talk in a relaxed way about problems the students could face, from homesickness to unwanted pregnancy. Adam half listened, but he was also aware of some kind of disturbance upstairs, a banging and a shouting. He thought he heard the Head's name. If Mo Highton was aware of the disturbance, she didn't let it affect her talk, which was drawing to an end.

"So I'll speak with each of you individually in the next week. I ought to tell you that I'm not here every day. I do some work for schools in Halifax, as well. But I'm available in the teachers' cottage most weekends and evenings. You can talk to me, privately, at any time."

The talk was over. The students made their way back to the dorms for their first dinner. Mo put a hand on Adam's shoulder.

"You're the oldest of this year's intake, Adam. That gives you some extra responsibility, too."

"If you say so."

"Why don't you make friends with Matthew over there?"

She was pointing at the boy with the owlish spectacles.

"He's shy, but he's very bright. I'm sure that you'd get on well together."

"Well, er . . ."

All of the new students had filed out. Mo and Adam were about to follow them, when Phil Merchant came running down the stairs.

"Wait!"

He spoke in a frantic whisper.

"I'd have gone for Mark and Simon, but they're helping with the meals. It's Kate. Nobody's seen her all day. I assumed she was in her office, meeting with parents. The phone was being answered earlier. But when I went up and knocked just now, there was no reply. I tried the door – it's locked – she never locks the office. I tried banging on the door. There was still no reply."

"Is there a spare key?" Mo asked.

Phil shook his head.

"I've never known her lock the door before."

"OK," said Mo, putting her arm lightly around Phil's waist. "Calm down. What do you want us to do?"

"There's only one thing we can do," Phil said, despairingly. "We have to force it open!"

They hurried up the stairs. Forcing the door was easier said than done. Kate's study had a heavy oak door. Mo held a finger to her lips so that Adam and Phil wouldn't speak. Then she began to talk.

"Kate, are you in there? Kate, it's me, Mo. Kate, we're worried about you . . . we think that you might have had an accident and not be able to speak. So, listen, Kate. We're going to have to force the door open to get to you. Don't worry. We'll try not to do too much damage. . . ."

She nodded at Phil and Adam. Then the three of

them barged the door with their shoulders. It wasn't a success. They hurt each other more than the door. They tried again. Still, it didn't budge.

"Let's try kicking it," Adam suggested.

Three feet slammed into hard wood. The door remained intact, but cracks appeared in the frame.

"Again!"

Splinters of wood came away from the frame. Adam's right foot hurt. He wished that he was still wearing his Doc Martens.

"Again!"

"Again!"

"Again!"

On the fifth go, the lock collapsed. The three of them were able to pull the door out of the frame. A bad smell was coming from the room they'd broken into. Phil Merchant went in first. He spoke.

"No. Not this."

Mo went in next.

"Oh god oh god oh god oh god oh god . . ."

She didn't stop. Adam followed her into the office. The Headteacher's body lay sprawled across her desk. Her head was soaked in blood.

"Why?" Phil Merchant asked. "Why did she do it?"

Mo shook her head. Adam felt surprisingly cool. He could see that both the adults were in shock, but he wasn't. He had hardly known Kate Dance. Phil Merchant went to pick up the phone.

"Don't touch it!" Adam snapped. "Don't touch anything. There might be fingerprints!"

He observed that the answerphone was switched on. That was why Phil had thought she was picking up the phone. Near her on the desk was a key, presumably the one to the office door.

"There's no need to get so excited," Mo told Adam patronisingly, all her former counselling tone gone. "It's obviously suicide. She shot herself in a locked room."

"In that case," Adam said, patiently, "perhaps you wouldn't mind telling me something. Where's the gun?"

6

Simon Lane was walking hurriedly from the boys' dorm. He looked annoyed.

"Adam, there you are. They've started eating dinner. You're going to miss yours. . . ."

Simon stopped, out of breath. For the first time, he seemed to notice that all was not well.

"Are you all right?"

Adam nodded.

"It's not me, it's . . ."

A police car appeared at the end of the rocky lane, its siren silent.

"Kate. She's dead."

All the colour went out of his father's face.

"How?"

"Somebody shot her."

Simon put his head in his hands.

"No. Not Kate. No."

Two policemen got out of the car. Simon looked devastated. Adam couldn't understand why his father was so upset. He couldn't have known the woman any better than Adam did. But there was one person who she must mean a lot to.

"Look, Simon – someone's got to tell Naomi. The other kids aren't to be told yet. Would you get her out of dinner? I'll talk to her."

"I don't know if . . ."

"Please."

"Well . . ." Simon didn't seem to be thinking clearly. "OK."

"I'll go over to your cottage."

Simon left as the police officers approached. Adam told them where to go. They wanted him to go with them, but he explained his errand, and agreed to be interviewed fifteen minutes later. Then he hurried over to the teachers' cottage. His mind was a blur. Who could have shot Kate Dance? And how could he tell Naomi that her aunt was dead? He had only known her for two days. But someone had to do it. Phil and Mo both seemed to be in shock.

"Adam?"

Naomi stood in the door. With make-up on, and figure-hugging clothes, she looked like an adult again.

"You'd better sit down."

Naomi shook her head and remained standing.

"What is it?"

Her impatience surprised Adam. He didn't know how to say what he had to say.

"Look, I'm sorry, er . . ."

"Adam, your father's just dragged me out of a dinner where I was talking to friends I haven't seen all summer. He said you had something important to tell me. Now, *what is it?*"

Adam blurted out the words.

"It's Kate, Naomi. She's dead."

"Dead?"

Naomi was staring at him in disbelief.

"She's been shot."

"Shot?"

Adam wasn't sure whether Naomi was asking him to confirm the fact or blankly repeating what he'd said.

"At first it looked like suicide, but there wasn't a gun. . . ."

He didn't want to say the word "murder". Naomi shook her head.

"Kate would never kill herself, not after . . . she wouldn't, that's all. Somebody murdered her."

"Yes," said Adam. "I'm afraid they did."

As Naomi stood there in shock, the kitchen door opened. Mark Rhodes, in jeans and polo shirt, looked in, an anxious expression on his face.

"I thought I'd better see what's going on. Your dad seemed in a right old state, Adam."

"It's not Simon."

Mark looked from Adam to Naomi, who spoke.

"Mark, it's Kate. Somebody shot her. She's dead."

Immediately, Mark put both his arms around Naomi, who collapsed onto his chest, crying her eyes out. Adam felt a twinge of envy. He should be the one holding her. Then he felt ashamed of himself. Mark had known her much longer. She needed a man at a moment like this, not a boy.

"I'd better go," he said to the English teacher. "The police want to see me." Then he added, "We're not meant to tell the other students."

Mark seemed to be in a daze.

"Thanks for helping, Adam."

Adam walked past the girls' dorm. The meal was over. All the students seemed to be laughing and chatting, oblivious to the absence of both the English teacher and the Head's niece. In the boys' dorm, they were still eating. Simon sat motionless at the centre table. He looked like Macbeth might have done after seeing Banquo's ghost. To his right sat Forrest, who was holding forth on some subject or other. He paused and everyone seemed to laugh. Was it genuine admiration the boys had for him, or was it that they feared him? Sometimes it was hard to tell the difference.

Adam had feared Forrest at first, but now his feelings had hardened into hatred. *He could have done it*, Adam thought. He had heard a noise like a shot last night, when Forrest was out. Adam knew of no motive for Forrest to have shot Kate, but he had no motive for shooting at Simon, two days ago, either. Maybe he was a psychopath.

Adam walked round to the boys' dorm door, opened it, and checked the corridor. There was no-one about. Everyone was where they were supposed to be, in dinner. As quietly as he could, Adam hurried down to the end room and opened the door. Expensive clothes were scattered across the bed. A calf-skin wallet lay open on the desk, with a thick seam of bank notes inside it. He opened the large wardrobe and felt for the loose stone at the bottom. There was a noise outside. Adam pressed himself into the wardrobe and prayed that it wasn't Forrest. Then a toilet flushed. Footsteps returned to the dining room. Pulling hard, Adam managed to remove a second stone. He felt in the cavity between the rooms. There was something there. He had to remove a third stone before he could pull the object out. It was a shotgun.

There was also a tin of pellets, but nothing else. Adam knew enough about guns to tell that Kate Dance had been killed by a bullet, not tiny pellets. Forrest was probably the one who shot at Adam and Simon in the Escort. But if he had shot and killed Kate Dance, he had an even better hiding place for his weapon and ammunition. Adam returned the shotgun to the cavity where he had found it. Then he put the stones back in place. He left as quickly as he could, already late for his interview with the police.

The murder squad were using Phil Merchant's study. Phil's room was a stark contrast to Kate's: all modern furniture and neat little notices. The only personal touch was a photo of his two children. No photo of his wife. They were divorced, Adam supposed, like his own mother and father.

"You helped kick the door in, I believe," Inspector Carter said.

"Yes."

"Had you been in the office before?"

"Once. Two days ago."

"And did you notice any changes since then?"

Adam thought for a moment. He was trying to work out how to introduce Forrest into the conversation. He remembered little about the room.

"Only the key on the desk. I don't think that was there before."

"You'd remember the key, would you, even though you'd only been in the room the once?"

Adam realised that it wasn't Forrest he should be thinking about. He might come under suspicion himself.

"I think Phil Merchant pointed out before that the room was never locked. He said there was no spare key. That was why I noticed it."

The Inspector appeared to accept this.

"Remember anything else?"

Adam stared at her for a moment. His interrogator was a plumpish woman with thick brown hair which curled around her neck. She had a thick Yorkshire accent.

"No. I'm sorry. I don't."

The Inspector scribbled a note.

"Can you account for your movements last night?"

"Is that when it happened?"

"When *what* happened?"

"The shooting."

"We don't know yet," said the Inspector. "We'll have to wait for the pathologist's report. However, we need to know who was here and what they were doing."

Adam had no alibi, he realised. He'd been alone most of the evening.

"I had dinner with Kate and several other people. Then I went back to the dorm, watched TV, played some music and read a little. I went to bed about half eleven."

"So you saw no-one and heard nothing?"

"Well, not quite . . ."

Adam told the Inspector everything he knew about Forrest – the shotgun that was fired at the Escort, how the boy came and went through the window, the threats he made about what would happen if Adam revealed that he'd been there, and, finally, the noise in the night that could have been a shot. The Inspector didn't seem too impressed.

"A shotgun proves nothing. There are at least five hundred children under sixteen with shotgun licences. And we think Ms Dance was killed by a .38 revolver. But the boy was around last night, you're sure, and didn't want his presence known?"

"That's right."

"Is he still here?"

Adam told her about Forrest's arrival that afternoon.

"We'd better see him, then. You say his name's Forrest?"

"Yes."

The Inspector paused, then checked what appeared to be a list of the school's students.

"You mean Viscount Anthony Forrest?"

"Maybe. I suppose."

It hadn't occurred to Adam that Forrest might be some kind of aristocrat. Maybe that explained his popularity.

"Where will we find him?" Inspector Carter asked.

Adam told her. Then he left. Mo Highton was waiting outside Phil's office. She had obviously been crying. As Adam walked down the stairs, he heard Inspector Carter asking Mo if she'd mind coming back later. Adam remembered the row he'd overheard between her and Kate the night before last. Should he have told the Inspector about that? Maybe. But Naomi said at the time that it was nothing important. Now, he wanted to see Naomi again. He wanted to find out what she knew about Forrest.

There were several boys in the common room of the girls' dorm. Adam didn't understand why it was that boys and girls had separate common rooms at Beechwood Grange. But Naomi wasn't there.

Adam stood in the shadows outside the boys' common room and watched as a police officer fetched Viscount Forrest to be interviewed by Inspector Carter. Forrest stared at the officer in something like disbelief, then appeared to make a joke of it to his entourage. Next, Adam went to the teachers' cottage. Mark and Simon were sitting in the kitchen, drinking whisky.

"I was looking for Naomi," Adam told them.

"She's asleep," Mark said. "I've given her my bed. We can't have her going back to the dorm and the other girls seeing how upset she is."

"I gave her a couple of my sleeping pills," Simon told him. "She should be out until morning."

It was the first Adam knew that his dad took sleeping pills. But then, there were a lot of things he didn't know about his father.

"The police want to talk to both of you," he told Mark and Simon. "They're interviewing everyone who was here last night. They want you first, Mark."

Mark nodded and stood up.

"Do they know yet whether it was suicide or murder?"

"No."

"Was anything stolen?" Mark asked, as he opened the door.

"I don't think so," Adam told him. "The Inspector didn't say."

"Let's hope it was suicide," Mark said, "and that it can be kept quiet. The last thing the school needs is another scandal."

"Another?" Adam started to ask, but Mark was gone.

Now that they were alone, Adam told his father about Forrest.

"You're sure it was the same boy?"

"Positive. Do you know anything about him?"

Simon thought for a moment.

"Only that he's from a very old and very rich family. I believe his father, Lord Forrest, contributed a lot of money to the new teaching block. I'm meant to be getting his son through English GCSE. Kate told me to treat him the same as everyone else, but more so, if you see what I mean. He has a lot of influence over other students. I think there's some trouble in his background. But that's not unusual. Lots of the kids here have been in bother with their old schools. I don't know what Forrest's particular crime was."

"Who would know?" Adam asked.

"Kate. Mo. Phil, probably. But I shouldn't be telling you this much. I don't know the lad. Kate seemed to think he was all right, when you really got to know him."

They sat and talked for a while longer, going over the events of the day. After a while, Mo returned.

"Do they want me now?" Simon asked.

"Not till they're through with Mark," Mo told him. "Don't go yet."

Adam sensed that Mo wanted to talk to Simon alone. It was time for him to leave. He walked through the moonlit night. The only noise was the gentle rush of the river and an occasional owl. Even the dorm was quiet. Adam went straight to his room and switched on the light. Nothing happened. It must have blown. Adam went over to put on the light by his study desk. Awkwardly, he reached over and fumbled for the switch.

That was when they got him. Before he knew what was going on, Adam was knocked to the floor. A sweaty sock was forced into his mouth. In silence, several boys held his arms and legs. Kicks rained on to his body, where the bruises wouldn't show so easily. It was agony. Adam had been done over before, but never so thoroughly, so professionally. When they'd finished, a torch was shone in his face.

"I told you I'd kill you," a familiar voice hissed. "Next time I will."

Adam was silent. Forrest pulled the wet sock from his mouth.

"Why did you tell the police where I was? What were they here for? Drugs, was it?"

Adam shook his head.

"I can't tell you."

"You told them I was a thief. You think I need to steal?"

"You took my CDs."

Forrest laughed.

"Here, between us, all property is theft. What's yours is mine."

"Very convenient," Adam told him.

Forrest sneered.

"You screwed up, Lane. I don't know what I'm supposed to have done last night, but it couldn't have been me. I took the eight o'clock train to Edinburgh yesterday evening. Dozens of people saw me on it. You tried to incriminate me, but only succeeded in making yourself look foolish. You've got a lot of learning to do, haven't you?"

Adam stayed silent. But he was confused. If Forrest didn't do it, who did?

"Teach him, boys."

Forrest's henchmen began to kick him again.

7

Next morning, the boys' dorm was noisy with rumours about why the police were in school. Most people believed it was a drugs raid, but some of the other suggestions going round made Adam's ears curl. His body was still aching all over from the night before. Adam had no energy to strike up conversations with the raucous strangers around him. He was glad when Simon came to say that he was needed in the Grange.

The police wanted Adam for fingerprinting. The process took only a few seconds, and the ink washed off easily. Even so, it made Adam feel like a criminal. They also fingerprinted the five other people who had been in the school grounds at eleven the night before last, which was the approximate time of death. They were: Phil Merchant, Simon Lane, Mark Rhodes, Mo Highton and Naomi Dance.

The three teachers who shared the cottage had gone to bed before the time of death, so none of them could give the others an alibi. It seemed that the police accepted Forrest's alibi. He wasn't fingerprinted. Adam wondered whether the Viscount's father had anything to do with the polite treatment which his son received. No press announcement of the Head's death was to be made until the next day. That was when the police expected to have finished their initial investigation. However, Phil Merchant decided that he could not put off telling the students what had happened. He announced it at morning assembly. The whole school was crammed into the small hall where the newcomers had been welcomed the night before.

"You'll all be wondering why the police are here this morning," Phil said, and the room immediately became silent. "I'm afraid that I have terrible news for all of you. Yesterday, Kate, our Headteacher, was found collapsed at her desk. She had died the previous night."

Adam looked around him. The most rebellious characters appeared shocked. Even Forrest, who was so arrogant, seemed to register alarm. Adam could barely stand, his body ached so much. Now the bully knew why Adam had had to inform on him.

"We don't yet know the cause of Kate's death," Merchant continued. "It seems likely that it was a tragic accident. . . ."

Does he really think that, Adam wondered? Or is he saying it so as not to scare the students? He looked around for Naomi, to see her reaction. But she wasn't there. Still asleep, he supposed. Mo and Mark stood next to Adam's father. None of them looked like they had slept much. Neither had he. Phil Merchant went on to give a eulogy to Kate Dance. He described her own education at Beechwood in the sixties, the work she had done in deprived London schools, the years she spent doing voluntary service in Africa.

"Education wasn't just her vocation, it was her whole life," Merchant said. "She didn't share her life with one person, as most of us do, but with all the students she taught. I know that, when she was appointed Head of the Grange School two years ago, she saw it as the culmination of all her ambitions. It was a job that she did superbly, quickly restoring the school's reputation after an unsettled period."

Merchant paused. Adam wondered about the "unsettled period" which he'd just referred to. What had happened then? He looked around him. Many of the students in the hall were openly crying. So was Mo Highton. Merchant's own voice was racked with emotion.

"The funeral cannot be arranged until the coroner's report is made, which may not be for several days. When it does take place, the school will close for the day, so that those who wish to can attend. Until then, though, school will go on as normal. That is what Kate would have wanted. She would have told you that learning to live with grief is part of life. . . ."

With that, he broke down, and had to wipe his eyes before he could finish.

"To help us with that grief, I would like us now to have a minute's silence."

But the minute wasn't silent. Every one of the students cried, even Forrest, even those who had only arrived the day before. Adam watched them coldly, feeling distanced from all the grief around him. Then he realised that the tears dripping onto his shirt were his own.

Jeff Porter, the history teacher, listened to Adam describe the course he'd been following in Ealing.

"Doesn't sound like you learned much," he said.

"I couldn't see the point of learning about the American West, or the causes of the First World War. They're hardly relevant to me."

"No? Well, we'll find you a different syllabus to follow, if that's what you want. But please bear in mind, it's not the subject that matters, it's the skills you learn to deal with it. . . ."

He picked up a pile of documents and put them into a plastic wallet.

"These are all reports about a famous scandal which took place in France, last century. I want you to compile me a report saying what, as far as you are able to find out, really happened. It must be no more than two sheets of A4 long and, at the end of it, you must cite your source for every single fact that you quote. Understood?"

"I guess."

"Good. See me if you have any problems. Otherwise, I'll see you at the same time next week. Have it finished by then."

Adam guessed that this was what they meant by "independent learning". It looked like easy work for the teachers. Adam didn't have another lesson until after lunch. As he was leaving the teaching block, he saw Naomi walking towards the girls' dorm, still wearing the clothes she'd had on the previous night. She looked spaced out.

"How are you?" Adam asked.

"OK." Naomi stared at the ground. "The doctor came and gave me some tranquillisers."

She met Adam's eyes for the first time.

"What about you? You look lousy."

"I slept badly, that's all."

There was no point in telling her about Forrest, now that the boy had a cast-iron alibi.

"Look," said Naomi, "I've got a geography tutorial in a few minutes, but come and see me later. I'd like to spend some time with you. Come to the dorm, after dinner."

"I'd like that."

Naomi gave Adam a blank smile then walked off, slowly. When she was out of sight, he debated what to do. He thought about going to the library and making a start on his history papers. When it came to it, though, he couldn't be bothered. Instead, he decided to go for a walk by the river. It was a glorious day. Mark Rhodes was sitting in the picnic area with a bunch of kids who'd been at the new students' meeting yesterday. They were playing with balloons.

"Hey, Adam, come here!" Mark called.

Adam went. The balloons, he saw, each had a word, letter, or short phrase written on them, like: "Jimmy says", "shoes", "where is", "I", "Sarah", "thanks", "yes", "and the". They made no sense to Adam.

"I'll bet you understand punctuation, don't you, Adam?"

Actually, Adam was lousy at it, but he nodded anyway.

"We're playing this game," Mark grinned. "Perhaps you'd help us."

The idea was to form sentences by holding up the balloons. Points were scored – not on the number of words used, but on the number of punctuation marks. Every time they needed a comma or a speech mark or a full stop, one of the kids had to draw it on a balloon, then blow it up. Each team then held up the balloons to form a sentence. Mark split the kids into two teams, with him helping one side and Adam the other. Thankfully, Tanya the self-confessed arsonist was on Mark's side. The game was silly, but it was fun. Adam's main problem was stopping the kids bursting the balloons before they'd finished making a sentence. In the end, Adam was sure that his team had won, when they made "Yes, thanks, I'd like one of Sarahs' shoes." But Mark docked them a point for putting an apostrophe in the wrong place. So it was a tie. All the kids on Adam's team blamed him.

"Don't worry about it," Mark said. "If the game didn't end up a draw, I'd be accused of encouraging competitive sports. Thanks for your help."

As Adam escaped, the kids engaged in an orgy of balloon bursting. Mark did nothing to stop them.

Adam walked past the teaching block back towards the dorm. In the science lab, a group of older students seemed to be fiddling with bunsen burners and chemicals, with no teacher present. A French language tape could be heard from another classroom. None of this seemed so different from his old school, except that there were so few students in each class. Adam guessed that there would be even less as term went on, when the kids got bored and used their freedom to opt out of lessons.

Adam decided to go to the Grange. He didn't want to run into Forrest in the dorm. Inside the old building, various sessions were taking place. Through an open door, Adam saw his father sitting on a table with half a dozen kids looking up to him. They appeared to be reading a play. When Simon saw Adam, he waved. Adam felt a twinge of guilt. Simon probably thought that Adam was skiving off. Adam went to the library, where he sat at one of the tables and opened his pack of history papers. They were about some French Army officer called Alfred Dreyfus. At least they were in English. Adam had flunked French and wasn't looking forward to retaking it.

"Hey, Adam!"

It was Tanya. She was wearing a bright yellow "Boy Toy" T-shirt.

"Wasn't that a brilliant game?"

"Is your session over already?"

"Nah. I got bored and opted out. That's what you're allowed to do here, right?"

"I guess."

"Are you doing 'A' levels?"

"No. GCSEs. Retakes."

Tanya gave him a grin which made her look even more ugly.

"So you're a dumbo, like me?"

"If you say so."

Adam picked up his papers to indicate that he was working.

"Actually, Tanya, I don't think you're meant to talk in the library."

"No way. You can do what you want in this place. That's what my mum said. Anyhow, we're the only people in here."

She had followed him, Adam realised, as soon as the punctuation game was over.

"Bummer about the Headteacher, huh? A lot of the girls are really upset. Know what they're saying?"

"No."

Tanya leant forward and whispered conspiratorially.

"They're saying that she killed herself because of some bloke. He was two timing her."

"She didn't . . ."

Adam stopped himself. He wasn't meant to reveal that he knew anything about Kate's death. And Tanya was the last person he should talk to. She was obviously a keen gossip.

"Some of them reckon she was seeing that English teacher, Mark Rhodes."

Adam couldn't conceal his disbelief.

"You're kidding! He's in his early twenties. She must have been forty."

Tanya shrugged.

"Don't ask me. I'm new here. But the school's got a reputation for sex, hasn't it? The girls all reckon that Rhodes stayed here in the summer because he had a little love nest going with the Head. Then his girlfriend – that woman from last night, the school counsellor – came back and told him to finish with her. So he did."

Adam tried to work out whether this theory fitted with the row he had overheard between Kate and Mo.

"Still," Tanya went on, "your dad's living with both of them now. I expect you know the full story."

Tanya leant forward so that she was nearly touching him. He could smell her deodorant.

"I can keep a secret," she told him.

"I'm afraid I don't know any."

Adam picked up a document called *J'Accuse* by Emile Zola, and pretended to be reading it. He heard Tanya get up and walk off, in a huff. But Adam couldn't read the words in front of him. His head was buzzing. He was sure now that Forrest hadn't killed Kate Dance. But, if Tanya was correct, there was one person in the school who had a motive to get rid of the Head – the teacher who'd been crying crocodile tears at the assembly that morning: Mo Highton.

8

Since Adam didn't know where Naomi's room was, he went to the girls' common room after dinner. It was more colourful than the boys' room, but just as shabby, and nearly deserted. At one side of the room, a group of girls, including Tanya, were watching *Coronation Street*. Two other girls, one white, one Afro-Caribbean, were talking by a window.

"I'm looking for Naomi Dance," Adam said to them. "Can you tell me which her room is?"

"Hers is the one which looks like a suite at the Hilton," the white girl sneered, in an American accent.

"Lay off Naomi. You're just jealous," said the other girl. Then she turned to Adam. "I think Naomi wants to be left alone. When her friends tried to comfort her about Kate, she gave them the cold shoulder."

Adam nodded. It sounded to him like Naomi was still in shock.

"Well, she's expecting me."

The black girl shrugged, then got up and pointed out which was Naomi's room. Adam knocked on the door.

"Come in."

Adam saw what the American girl had meant about the Hilton. Naomi had a wooden single bed, not a tatty bunk like his. There was a complex patchwork quilt over it. She also had framed posters on the wall and an antique roll-top desk. In the corner of the room were her own TV and video.

"This is nice," he said.

Naomi shrugged. She was at her desk, wearing a Japanese silk kimono.

"I'm hardly ever at home, so I brought some of my things with me."

She stood up.

"You'd better wait for me in the common room. If you have a boy in your room when you're dressed like this, people talk."

She smiled – the first proper smile Adam had seen her give since Kate's death. He went and sat at the back of the common room, where he watched the beginning of *Brookside*. When Naomi joined him, she wore jeans and a rugby shirt.

"How are you feeling?"

"So so," Naomi told him. "I keep going over what happened in my mind. I don't think I'll be able to relax properly until I know how Kate died."

"That's what I wanted to talk to you about."

Naomi leant closer to him and lowered her voice.

"Why, did the police tell you something?"

"No, but I know what I saw. Kate was murdered."

Naomi shook her head.

"Who would do a thing like that? No-one had a reason to."

Adam explained his theory about Mo killing Kate. Naomi laughed.

"Mark and Kate? You must be kidding. I was here over the summer. I'd have noticed. The argument you overheard was just another of those education things. Teachers love to get on their high horse about any old issue. You must have noticed that."

She was patronising him.

"Do you have a better theory?" Adam asked, snidely.

"Maybe," Naomi said. "You keep going on about the missing gun. Maybe whoever found her body took away the gun. Has that occurred to you?"

"But I was there."

Naomi explained patiently.

"Suppose that you weren't really the first to find her? Suppose Phil Merchant got in earlier, took the gun and somehow locked the door?"

Adam was confused.

"Why would he do that?"

"Because he didn't want it to look like she killed herself. Some people are funny about suicide, you know."

Adam remembered something.

"Last night, you told me that you were sure Kate wouldn't kill herself."

Naomi shrugged this off.

"Did I? I was in a bit of a state last night."

Adam thought for a moment. It was possible that

someone close to Kate – Mark Rhodes perhaps – had not wanted it known that she'd committed suicide. Naomi's hypothesis would fit with Tanya's theory, too. But it wasn't complete.

"If someone removed the gun, how do you explain the locked door?"

Naomi shook her head.

"I've thought about that a lot today. Nothing fits with the locked door – certainly not your theory that Mo did it because Kate was having an affair with Mark."

"It wasn't my theory, it was . . . oh, never mind."

Adam tried to concentrate. It was hard, given his lack of sleep and the bruises which still made his whole body ache.

"Suppose . . ."

Naomi interrupted him.

"Suppose you let the police work it out? You're starting to upset me, Adam."

"I'm sorry."

A bunch of loud girls about Adam's age came in from the games room, sweat still glistening on their foreheads. One of them bought cans of cold Coke from the machine in the corner. Without asking, another went over to the television, turned up the sound, and switched channels to MTV. From another part of the room, a loud, familiar voice complained.

"Hey! I was watching that!" It was Tanya. "Turn it back!"

The four girls sat themselves down right in front of the TV set. The tallest one turned round and sneered.

"Don't you know the school rules? Whenever Paul Nelson's on television, we have to watch him."

"What rules? Why?"

The girl raised her eyebrows and wobbled her eyes to indicate that Tanya was ga-ga.

"Because he used to come here, that's why."

With that, Tanya, realising that she was outnumbered, gave up. The concert, a live telecast from the Expo Arena in Seville, had already begun. Paul Nelson was in the middle of a guitar solo. To Adam's surprise, Naomi started to watch it. She hushed him when he tried to talk again. Maybe she preferred the bland music to his conspiracy theory conversation. Nelson had a large band: two guitars, bass, keyboards, two drummers and a brass section. He played mainly his hits from the last few years. When he did the old numbers that Adam liked, the Call to Arms songs, they sounded just like the others, only with more guitar. It was depressing to watch. Adam would have gone off to do something else, but he didn't want to desert Naomi. In the middle of the concert, nine of the ten-piece band left the stage. Only the piano player and the singer remained. Nelson waited for the audience to quieten down. Then he stepped into the single spotlight and spoke in a hushed voice.

"I'd like to do a song in memory of a good friend of mine who died this week. This is for Kate Dance."

As the piano introduced the plaintive tune, the throb of noise in the common room disappeared. Nelson began to sing an old Call to Arms' number, *Water's Edge*. The song was a warning: sometimes, if you went into things too deeply, you ended up drowning. Adam knew the song by heart, but the way Nelson was singing it tonight, the words took on new meaning. Adam wondered how the singer had found out about Kate's death. It hadn't been in the news yet. Then he heard a noise from behind him. When he looked round, Naomi had gone.

Adam got up to go after her. Several girls shushed him as he hurried out into the corridor. He looked into her room. It was empty. He headed for the exit door. Then he heard heavy footsteps. Someone was following him. He turned round, thinking that it might be Naomi, that she had just popped out to the toilet, or something. But it wasn't. It was short, dumpy Tanya.

"I wasn't enjoying the concert, either. Can I come to the boys' common room with you? We're only allowed in there if we're somebody's guest."

"I'm not going there."

"Where are you going, then?"

"I don't know."

Tanya followed him out into the open. She showed no sign of going away. Exasperated, Adam snapped at her.

"Look, stop pestering me, will you? You're a pain in the backside."

"And you're a . . ."

Adam didn't stick around to hear the expletive. He had seen something in the trees, on the other side of the river — a pale colour which could have been Naomi's blouse. He hurried to the narrow bridge and crossed the river. Then he charged into the wood. The tall beech trees were still in leaf, reducing what little light came from the clouded sky. Adam had been in the woods before, on his walk with Naomi two days ago, but then it had been daylight. Now, he couldn't find the path. He thought he heard a rustling noise in the distance.

"Naomi?"

Perhaps it was better not to call her. After all, if she had wanted him with her, she had only to say so. Perhaps Nelson's song had upset Naomi and she wanted to be alone. Adam moved towards the noise more cautiously. After a few minutes, he found the path which led through the woods. Now it was possible to walk quickly without making a noise. Adam could hear two voices: one male, one female. When Adam was near enough to hear what they were saying, he stopped. He recognised both voices, and didn't want them to know that he was there.

"What are you telling me all this for?" the female voice asked, impatiently. "If you've worked it out, you should realise that I know it all already."

"Because you're responsible," said the male voice, "and I'm not. You're going to have to decide what to do about it."

"And if I don't do anything more than I've already done?"

"Then I guess I'll have to go to the police."

An owl began to hoot overhead and Adam couldn't follow the woman's soft-voiced reply. The final words he heard were from the boy.

". . . by tomorrow night. Meet me here, at the same time."

Heavy footsteps started coming in Adam's direction. Hurriedly, he stepped back into the trees. He was just in time. Viscount Anthony Forrest walked past him very quickly. Adam stayed in his hiding place for a couple of minutes, waiting for the woman to come, too. But she didn't.

Adam's sore muscles were stiffening up. He had to move. Slowly, carefully, he walked along the path to where the conversation had taken place. As he did so, the wind picked up. A cloud which had covered the moon rolled away from it, casting light through the branches of the trees below. And Adam saw her. She sat on a tree stump, with her head in her hands, wearing a light-coloured dufflecoat, her mousy hair drooping over it: the woman who had killed Kate Dance.

It was Mo Highton.

9

Adam walked back to the dorm, trying to figure out the meaning of what he had overheard. Forrest, Adam supposed, had seen or heard *something* while he was hiding at the school. Now he was using what he'd found out to blackmail Mo about the killing. That was in character. Why would Forrest give the police the information when he could make his own mischief with it? If Adam had understood the conversation correctly, it didn't look like Mo was about to confess. So what should Adam do? He could tell the police. But Forrest would deny it, making Adam look foolish. He'd say that Adam had a grudge against him – after all, Adam had informed on him once already. Adam could tell his father. Or he could confront Forrest himself.

Exhausted and unsure what action to take, Adam

decided to lie down for a few minutes. His body ached all over. Back in his room, he switched on the light, forgetting that Forrest had broken it the night before. He stumbled over to switch on the desk lamp. Then, slowly, painfully, he lifted himself onto the top bunk. Halfway up, he stopped, abruptly. Somebody was already in the bed. It was Naomi. She was sleeping like a baby. Her face looked so peaceful in the dim light, Adam couldn't bring himself to wake her. Naomi hadn't run out on him, after all. She'd been upset by the concert, so had come to his room and waited for him to arrive. Pleased, Adam decided to wait for her to wake up. When she did, they could discuss what to do about Mo and Forrest. Once he told her what he had heard in the woods, she was bound to be convinced Mo was responsible for Kate's death.

Leaving the light on, he lay down on the lower bunk. The mattress was useless, but he was too tired to notice. For a few seconds he listened to Naomi's gentle, steady breathing from the bunk above. Then he fell fast asleep. When Adam woke, it was morning. Pale sunshine streaked through the blind above his desk. His back ached. It took him a few moments to remember where he was and why he was sleeping on such an uncomfortable bed. Then he remembered.

"Naomi?"

Awkwardly, he pulled himself out of bed and stood up. The top bunk was empty. He looked around. On the desk, his student's notepad was open. There was a felt-tipped pen beside it, with the top missing. The note was in large letters, printed in red ink. Naomi's writing was rounded and wobbly, almost childish:

Adam,
I really needed someone to talk to but it seems like we couldn't manage to be awake at the same time. I'll see you at the meeting.

love,
Naomi
X

Someone knocked on Adam's door. He hoped that it would be her.

"Come in."

It was Matthew, the thin boy in owlish spectacles whom Mo Highton had tried to persuade Adam to pal up with.

"Sorry to disturb you, Adam, but I couldn't find you last night. Today's Friday – you're on breakfast duty every Friday this term. We're meant to be in the kitchen in ten minutes."

"OK. Thanks."

Breakfast duty didn't sound too bad. You had to collect the milk, put out various bowls for cereal and muesli, make tea, coffee and endless toast. If anyone wanted a cooked breakfast, they had to do it themselves. Adam felt better for his ten hours sleep. The bruises all over his body were starting to fade, and he felt only a little stiff now. When he got to the kitchen, Matthew had already put on the urn and was sorting out cups. Adam began to load the giant toaster.

"Why'd you come to this school?" he asked Matthew.

"My parents thought it would do me good to have a year here before going back to University."

"*University*? How old are you?"

"Fifteen. They've accepted me to do a PhD, but they won't let me start until I'm sixteen."

Adam's mind boggled.

"So that means you've already got a degree?"

"Yes. I got a first in biochemistry at King's, Cambridge. What I really want is to make a major contribution to medical science by the time I'm eighteen."

The boy's voice was very matter of fact. Adam wasn't sure whether he should be irritated by Matthew's arrogance or applauding his ambition.

"How do you plan to do that?"

"Molecular biology is where all the really interesting work is going on at the moment. I'm going to study gene expression in patients suffering from muscular dystrophy."

Adam thought about asking for an explanation, but decided that he was out of his depth.

"By the way," Matthew said, "you might want a look at this."

This was that morning's copy of the *Yorkshire Post*, which was delivered to the common room. The front page was dominated by Kate's death.

HEAD TEACHER SLAIN AT "FREE SEX" SCHOOL

Adam read the article below the headline. The first paragraph was about the circumstances surrounding Kate's death. But the second was news to him.

> *Ms Dance was appointed Head at the Free School two years ago in the wake of a scandal which dominated the tabloid press for days. According to reports from a*

"mole", soft drugs, teenage pregnancies and sexually transmitted diseases were rife in the school. Many parents withdrew their children in the wake of the scandal. Several teachers, including the Head, were asked to leave by the governors.

On her appointment, Ms Dance, a former pupil of the school, curtailed the school's notorious sex education policy, brought in new members of staff and boosted academic standards. She also instituted separate common rooms for boys and girls, ending the school's "free sex" image.

Her deputy, Philip Merchant, felt that Ms Dance had succeeded in turning the school around after its near collapse. "Her death is a tragedy," he told us. From a stage in Seville, her former classmate, Paul Nelson, dedicated his song, Water's Edge to her.

"Did you know any of this sex scandal stuff?" Adam asked Matthew.

"Of course," said Matthew. "It's common knowledge. It's the first thing everyone asks the older students about. They're still trying to work out who leaked the story to the press two years ago."

Adam realised that the only older student who he'd really talked to was Naomi, and she had arrived after the scandal. Now he understood some aspects of the school better – the separate common rooms, the hints his father had dropped about the Grange "not being like that any more".

Adam got on with pouring mugs of tea. The other boys started to arrive for breakfast. Matthew and Adam's job was nearly over. They only had to make sure that the toast didn't run out, which was easy, because the giant toaster held eighteen slices at once. Adam guessed that Mo Highton had fixed for the two of them to be on the same rota. But he couldn't hold that against Matthew, who seemed like a nice bloke. It wasn't his fault that he was frighteningly clever.

Jobs finished, they began to talk again. Matthew told him about the arts and languages courses he was going to do at the Grange. Kate Dance had been going to teach him to paint. Mark Rhodes was giving him tuition in creative writing. Adam told Matthew about his old band.

"Do you like music?" he asked the younger boy.

"I always wanted to play drums," Matthew told Adam. "But I never had time. I've got a stereo, but I don't have much to play on it."

"You can come to my room later," Adam said. "I'll lend you some CDs."

"Great."

They sat down to eat their muesli. As Adam was finishing the toast, Forrest walked in. Breakfast was meant to be over by nine. It was five past.

"There's no toast left," Forrest moaned. "Who's on?"

Hands pointed at Adam and Matthew.

"In future," Forrest snarled, "save me three slices. And make me some now."

Matthew got up to do it.

"No," said Adam. "Leave it. Let him make his own."

"It's no problem."

Matthew turned the giant toast machine back on. It was a rotating rack nearly a metre long, with six sides and a long toaster element in each. Adam had switched the machine off only moments before, so it heated up quickly. It infuriated Adam, seeing this kid who was worth a hundred Forrests being pushed around by the bully.

"Leave it, Matthew. I'll deal with him."

Adam went back behind the kitchen counter. There were four slices of bread left in the plastic wrapper. Adam took them out.

"Feeling better today?" Forrest sneered.

Adam took the four bits of bread to the bowl where the boys slopped their unfinished cereal. He dropped them in.

"Oh dear," he said, sarcastically. "What a waste. Still, accidents happen."

It was a petty gesture, but it made him feel better. Forrest glared at him.

"You're right," he told Adam. "Accidents happen."

He looked around him.

"And I've got a roomful of witnesses to explain how this one happened."

With that, Forrest picked up the huge toaster by its insulated sides. The six elements glowed a violent orange. Forrest lifted the toaster above his head. Trapped behind the counter, Adam could only watch as the burning hot machine came crashing down towards him.

"Put that down *now*!"

Mark Rhodes charged across the room until he was standing between Adam and Forrest. Reluctantly, Forrest put the machine back where it had come from. Rhodes pulled out the plug. Then he began to shout.

"Get to Phil Merchant's office. Immediately."

Forrest left. Mark addressed the seven other boys who were still in the dining area.

"I'm ashamed of you. We teach you to take responsibility for each other. Yet not one of you tried to stop that lout attacking Adam. I don't care what the provocation was. Violence is *never* justified. Have you got that? *Never!*"

The boys walked out, faces to the floor. Mark turned to Matthew and Adam.

"What happened?"

Matthew told him. Mark shook his head.

"You don't mess around with people like him," he told Adam. "You can't win. I know of at least three lads who've left the school because of him. The last one was called Steven Crosby – his mother rang up yesterday to say why she hadn't brought him back. She said that, since the year he'd spent here, he'd begun wetting his bed and developed a severe facial twitch. She didn't mention Forrest. She didn't have to."

"Can't you get rid of him?"

Rhodes shook his head.

"He was thrown out of five public schools before he came here. But the Grange has a tradition – no-one has ever been expelled. Kate wouldn't change that. Only the students could. And Forrest is popular with quite a few of them. This is supposed to be his last year."

"It's my only year," Adam complained.

Mark put his hand on Adam's shoulder.

"That's tough." He continued, "I came to remind you that it's the first meeting of School Council in twenty minutes. The whole school's usually there for the first meeting. It's the one where the school rules are agreed."

"Don't you mean *guidelines*?"

"No," said Mark. "I don't."

10

The atmosphere in the hall was subdued. The room seemed to be awash with jeans and baggy T-shirts. No-one wanted to stand out. The students had dressed down so successfully, Adam thought, that they had almost succeeded in creating a school uniform, one that even the teachers wore. There was an order of precedence, too. The older kids sat near the front. The very young ones were at the back. The teachers were on one side of the hall. Adam sat on the other, in the middle, by the door, with Matthew next to him.

Just as the meeting was beginning, Naomi arrived. She wore a pink T-shirt which read "This used to be my playground". A black girl of about seventeen stood up.

"I'm Wanda. If it's OK with everyone, Phil asked me to start," she said. "The way this meeting works is simple. We review the guidelines from previous years, deciding whether to keep them or not. Then we discuss any new ones which are proposed. We will try to keep as few guidelines as possible. However, we must also obey the law: so, no drugs, no drinking at the pubs in the village, no weapons of any kind."

Adam, still seething from the attack earlier, interrupted. "What do we do if someone's got a shotgun?" he asked. "If, for instance, I knew that a certain Viscount kept a gun in a hole behind his wardrobe and had shot at me and my father with it?"

Wanda was silent. Phil Merchant spoke.

"That's a serious allegation. If it's more than hypothetical, you'd better see me afterwards."

Adam laughed bitterly. "If no-one goes for the gun now, it'll be gone as soon as we get out."

An Asian girl from the front spoke firmly. "And if someone *were* to find a gun there, how could we be sure it wasn't planted? Come *on*. This isn't the place to pursue a personal vendetta."

Adam knew that he had stirred it up as much as he could. He shut up.

"OK," said Wanda. "I propose that we keep the following guidelines: no fighting outside the gym; people caught stealing or bullying to get detentions decided by, and run by, students; no smoking in the school buildings apart from bedrooms and the smoking areas of common rooms."

No-one argued. Then there were the proposals for new guidelines. A German boy wanted the cooking and cleaning rotas to be more heavily weighted to the younger students.

"The people with GCSEs and 'A' levels to prepare for don't have time. I know it's supposed to be 'character building', but, after four years, I think my character's been built enough. I'd rather do academic work."

Now the younger students came into their own. They protested fiercely. Tanya was the first of the new students to speak.

"I agree with the others – you're being ageist. No-one would take you seriously if you proposed that only the girls did the domestic jobs. Why should age be any different? Also, you might have been doing it for four years, but other people only join the school when they're older – like me, or Adam over there. Why should we get out of having to do it?"

There was some applause for Tanya. Everyone looked over at Adam again, embarrassing him. Wanda concluded that there was no consensus for a change in the rota systems. She pointed out that allowances were already made for people on the day of their exams. Then she asked for the next point. Forrest stood up.

"I'd like to propose that the school has a guideline which prevents the teaching staff from enrolling their own children as students here."

There was a small gasp. Forrest went on.

"I don't wish to talk about individuals, but this has only happened in the last couple of years, and I think it needs to be nipped in the bud. I know that several teachers have children who don't come here. But when they do, they create a separate class of students, a divisive group – one that's too close to the teaching staff for comfort."

"He's having a go at me, too," Naomi whispered. "Don't let him get to you. He's a creep."

But Adam could hear several murmurs of agreement around the room.

"There's a tendency," Forrest went on, "for the children of teachers to become informers. No matter how equal a school is, there will always be conflicts between teachers and students. It's the nature of things. But what happens when you've got a student who sides more with the teachers? Let me give you a personal example."

He leant forward and lowered his voice, as though addressing each student in the room confidentially.

"I've got a girlfriend in the village – Jenny – it's not a secret to my friends, but it is to my parents. They wouldn't like it. So, in order to see her in the holidays, I pretended to be on a retreat in Scotland, but actually spent the week here, hanging around the school."

He paused and glanced over at the teachers.

"Interesting place, the school, when people think they're alone. Anyway, I went up to Scotland at the end of the week and thought that was the end of it. Only, then, someone reports me – gets me in bother with the police, who need to tell my parents, who find out about Jenny and stop me seeing her in the holidays again. . . ."

By now he was glaring at Adam. Adam sucked in air. In front of him, he saw that Naomi's face had turned white. Forrest smiled, and continued to talk in a reasonable tone. "Now, personally, I don't have a shotgun. But, if I did, I'd be inclined to use it to get rid of the person who got me into that kind of bother."

There was a laugh at this. Forrest concluded.

"However, if we adopt this new guideline, it won't be necessary."

There was general applause and a few hoots of support. Then there were several speeches from other students. They said little beyond the fact that they supported Forrest. Adam stood up. Naomi pulled him down again.

"Don't speak yourself, Adam. You'll lose. Wait and see if anybody else supports you."

It was good advice. Sukvinder, the girl who had attacked Adam before, now had a go at Forrest.

"This is just more personal revenge stuff. Why don't you and Adam Lane go and talk it through with Mo if you've got a problem? You're wasting our time."

Next, Tanya rose to speak for the second time.

"First people want to discriminate on the grounds of age, now it's on the grounds of who your parents are. What's next, no children of criminals, 'cos they might be thieves? Or maybe no children of Lords and Ladies, 'cos they got all their money by ripping off common people!"

Matthew and a couple of the new kids applauded this. Everyone else was silent. Wanda waited a moment, then asked.

"Does anyone else want to speak against?"

"Don't the teachers get a say?" Adam whispered.

Naomi shook her head.

"They're only meant to give out information."

"Then I'd better say something."

"Don't. You've lost before you open your mouth."

"I think that nearly everyone agrees," Wanda said. "No teachers' kids."

"That's it?" Adam said, in a loud voice. "That's the debate?"

"You had your chance to speak," Wanda told him firmly. "There's a clear consensus. The new guideline's agreed."

Adam was nonplussed. Now Phil Merchant spoke.

"Of course, this guideline cannot be enforced retrospectively. It will only apply to new applications to join the school."

"That's not what I meant!" Forrest shouted.

But he was too late. Wanda was closing the meeting.

Outside, Adam tried to find Tanya to thank her for speaking for him. She was nowhere around. Simon came over.

"You've got a lot to learn about politics," he told Adam.

"That gun's still here, I know it."

"Yes, but *you* wouldn't have been if it weren't for Phil's fancy footwork. These are nice kids. How come you've made so many enemies?"

Adam shrugged.

"I wish I knew. Look. There's something else I need to talk to you about."

"Well, it'll have to wait until later. I'm meant to be teaching an English lesson, to your friend Forrest, amongst others."

Simon gave Adam a wry smile.

"He can't be as bad as all that, you know. The kids obviously like him. So do some of the staff. And the story about the girlfriend's true, according to Mo Highton. He has a right to feel aggrieved."

Adam didn't bother arguing.

"I need to see you on your own, before tonight."

"After dinner, then. I'm eating in the boys' dorm tonight."

Adam wasn't sure what to think about Mo. If he was right, Forrest was blackmailing her about the fact that she'd killed Kate Dance. Hence Mo would have to back up the girlfriend story. But maybe it *was* true. What other reason would Forrest have to hang about the school during the summer holidays? Adam decided to discuss it with Naomi.

She was in her room, studying. Adam glanced at the chaotic notes which were spread all over the desk and her patchwork quilt. They looked even more confused than his GCSE literature notes, and he'd only managed a "D".

"Have you read *Othello*?" she asked him.

Adam shook his head.

"It all made sense last term, but when I read it now, I get confused. I'm meant to have made notes on Act One before my tutorial tomorrow."

She closed the book and cleared a space for him to sit on the bed.

"Thanks for coming by, anyhow."

"There's some things I need to tell you."

Adam explained about the meeting he'd overheard the previous night. Naomi listened carefully.

"So Forrest was telling the truth when he said that he was around during the holidays?"

"Yes. But I don't know if the girlfriend bit's true."

"Oh, of course it is," Naomi said. "Half the school's seen him with Jenny. She works behind the bar in the Crown."

"I thought the guideline said no drinking in village pubs?"

"It doesn't apply to prospective peers of the realm."

"So what do you think we should do?" Adam asked her. "Do you believe me now when I tell you that Mo Highton probably killed Kate?"

Naomi was silent for nearly a minute.

"I can't see Mo as a murderess," she said, finally. "But then, I can't see who else had any motive, either. . . ."

"What shall we do about it?"

"We?"

Naomi gave him a stern glance.

"It was my aunt who died, not yours. And, from what you've said, you've messed with Forrest enough already. I think I ought to handle this."

Adam didn't like to disagree with her.

"What will *you* do, then?"

Naomi opened the main drawer in her desk. It was an even bigger mess than Adam's. She began to dig about in the jumble. Finally, she pulled out a tiny portable DAT machine, much fancier than anything Adam had seen before.

"Where'd you get that?"

She shrugged.

"It was a present, but I haven't used it yet. Help me figure out how to work it."

They tested the recorder. It picked up the smallest whisper from the other end of the room.

"How are you going to use it?" Adam asked.

"I'll wait for Mo in the woods tonight. When Forrest comes to see her, I'll record their conversation."

Naomi smiled.

"With any luck, we'll get enough to be rid of both of them."

Adam smiled more weakly.

"Look," he said. "I'm not happy about you going on your own. It's dangerous."

Naomi shook her head.

"You ought to listen to your little friend, Tanya. You're being sexist. You watched them last night. I'm going to watch them tonight. What's the difference?"

Adam was stumped for a reply.

"At least let me come with you."

"Then they'd be twice as likely to notice us. No, Adam. I'll be safe. I promise to let you know what happens as soon as I get back."

Adam had run out of arguments.

"OK."

Naomi kissed him on the forehead.

"Take care," he told her.

"Don't worry about me," she told him. "I'll be fine."

Outside, students were just finishing their first morning sessions. Adam passed Forrest and a bunch of his henchmen.

"Who've you been seeing?" The Viscount asked, with a Johnny Rotten sneer in his voice. "Naomi Dance? You want to watch her."

Adam lifted a fist, but stopped himself. The bully was trying to provoke him. Forrest walked off with his mates, all of them laughing. Adam continued towards the teaching block, thinking about what would happen in the woods tonight. *I can't do it*, he told himself, still feeling the softness of Naomi's first kiss on his forehead. *I can't let her go into the woods on her own.*

11

Tanya was walking towards the teaching block, alone. Adam guessed that she hardly knew anyone yet. The way she'd defended him at the school council meeting that morning wouldn't have made her many friends. He caught her up.

"I wanted to thank you for what you said at the meeting. I'm sorry I was nasty to you last night. I had things on my mind."

"Yeah. I know. Naomi Dance."

Tanya glared at him.

"I'll tell you how you can make it up to me," Tanya said. "Come to the theatre. Join our lesson."

"Drama?" Adam said. "I hate drama."

"No, it's an English lesson really. More stuff on punctuation."

"I don't . . ."

"Come on," Tanya urged him. "It'll be fun."

They were outside the theatre now, a small stone building which had once been the Grange's chapel. The wooden doors were open.

"Come on, Tanya. You're late!"

Mark Rhodes was wearing a green hippyish smock and tatty cords.

"Adam, good of you to come!"

Mark called cheerfully from the stage. He was handing out large cards, a metre square, which had parts of sentences written on them.

"I was just explaining to the class. Yesterday, we were writing punctuation marks. Today, we're going to *be* punctuation."

"OK," he announced to the dozen or so students. "There's a square each. First, I want you to take these phrases and construct a paragraph. Lay it out all over the stage!"

There was immediate chaos. Squares were moved every few seconds. Arguments broke out. Mark was forced to intervene in several squabbles. Adam, not having a square, stood on the edge of the stage, observing. Slowly, he began to make sense of the words jumbled in front of him, some of which were familiar:

> a sea of troubles   to sleep   To die   no more
> whether   or to take arms against   or not to be
> tis noble in the mind to suffer   to be
> And by opposing end them   that is the question
> the slings and arrows of outrageous fortune

Once Adam had the beginning, it was easy. He began to boss the kids about, so that the words appeared in the right order. He got confused in the middle, but Mark Rhodes encouraged him, until, finally, the words made sense.

"OK," said Mark. "That was the easy bit. Now you've got to work out the punctuation. But there's a catch. You've got to express the punctuation marks with *your bodies*."

The students groaned. Pluckily, Tanya immediately made herself into a question mark at the end of "To be or not to be".

"No," Adam shouted. "That's a colon."

"What on earth's a colon?"

Slowly, each student contorted themselves into a shape. Everyone had a role, because it took two to make the colons and semi-colons.

"Adam," Mark called out. "Since you've been so helpful, perhaps we could do with a full stop at the end."

Adam rolled himself into a tight ball on the cold stage floor.

"All right," said Mark. "Now, you might think that you've been learning punctuation, but I can guarantee that you've also just learnt your first bit of Shakespeare by heart. Without looking around, let's see if you can chant it to me."

Together, all fourteen of them began to recite:

"To be or not to be: that is the question:
Whether 'tis nobler in the mind to suffer
The slings and arrows of outrageous fortune,
Or to take arms against a sea of troubles,
And by opposing end them? To die: to sleep;
No more."

"Brilliant," Mark called out. "Have a rest."

As the students collapsed into giggles, Adam got up to go.

"So you do teach Shakespeare, after all," he said to Mark.

The teacher smiled.

"I teach it when I want to, not when the government tells me I have to." Adam left before Tanya could waylay him again. He was twenty minutes late for his French lesson. But what was the point of being in a school like this if you couldn't be spontaneous when you felt like it?

The French session was led by Thérèse Depigny, one of the teachers who lived outside the school. She ignored Adam's arrival, concentrating instead on speaking in French to Matthew. Adam asked one of the other students what they were meant to be doing.

"Dunno."

In a corner of the room, two students were sitting listening to something on headphones. There was a spare set, so Adam picked them up and listened to what appeared to be a French rock station. Unfortunately, each piece of music faded out, so that all you got was the DJ's prattle and the adverts. After a few minutes, Adam was bored. Thérèse Depigny showed no sign of noticing that Adam was there, so he left. He'd always hated French.

Lunch was a "help yourself" meal. Adam ate alone. Then he went up to the library and worked on his Dreyfus papers. It seemed that the Army officer had betrayed his country by delivering secret defence documents to a foreign power. Dreyfus claimed that he'd been framed. He was court martialled, found guilty and transported to Devil's Island for life. Adam found himself getting interested in the case. The facts didn't add up. When he looked at his watch, he found that he'd missed his science tutorial.

At dinner, Simon was angry with him.

"It's one thing to skip a session, as I gather you did with French today, but to miss a tutorial, where a teacher has set aside time especially for you . . . it's not on, Adam."

Adam was irritated – he wouldn't have to put up with this if his father wasn't a teacher at the school.

"I'll apologise to the teacher later. Look, Dad, I need to talk to you."

"We're talking, aren't we?"

"Privately."

"Come up to the cottage, then. There's only Mo there, and you're due to see her tonight, anyway."

"*What?*"

"She interviews all the new students. I think you're the only one she hasn't seen yet."

"But it was her I wanted to talk to you about."

"Oh, very well. Come with me now."

They went to the theatre, which Simon unlocked. Adam told Simon about Mark's punctuation lessons.

"Unorthodox, but quite clever," said Simon.

"What do you make of Mark and Mo?" Adam asked him.

"How do you mean?"

"Are they . . . you know . . . together?"

Simon raised an eyebrow.

"You mean, are they lovers? No, they're not. Mo has

a boyfriend in Halifax. She stays there quite often. What's got into you? Have you been reading all that 'school for sex' stuff in the papers?"

This annoyed Adam.

"Yes, I have. Why weren't you straight with me about all that?"

Simon frowned.

"As I understand it, there was nothing to be *straight* about. The school had some problems, but nothing that you wouldn't find in half the comprehensives in the country."

Adam wasn't convinced.

"Tell me what happened."

Simon shrugged.

"From what Kate told me, two-and-a-half years ago someone rang up the *News of the World*. They gave the newspaper a load of stories about the school. There was a smidgeon of truth in them, but they were all grossly exaggerated – sex, drugs, you name it. The tabloid press had a field day, but the only thing anyone could pin on the teaching staff was a bit too much tolerance – and for having an open, explicit sex education policy – which I agree with, incidentally.

"The upshot was that a lot of students left, along with some of the better teachers. The school governors felt that the school had lost all its credibility and asked the Head to resign. Kate got his job and made some changes to help the school's credibility. She brought in new teachers and introduced the separate common rooms business."

"Which staff are still here from before?"

"Just two, I think. Phil Merchant and Mo Highton."

Adam nodded.

"There's something I need to tell you about Mo."

Adam told Simon about the meeting he'd overheard between Forrest and Mo, then about the row between Kate and Mo on the night they'd arrived. Simon shook his head in disbelief.

"Have you told any of this to the police?"

"No."

"It's a good job. Phil Merchant's already talked to me about your feud with Forrest. You might not like him, Adam, but you have to live with him. I'm sure that the conversation you overheard has an innocent explanation."

"Like what?"

Simon's voice became more urgent.

"You're acting like this is a game. It's not. I don't know how, or why Kate died, and neither do you. The police have been going all over the Grange today, doing their fingerprinting. The caretaker's had to camp at the top of the lane to keep reporters out after that bloody rock star announced Kate's death on MTV. And now you're accusing the school counsellor of killing Kate in a jealous rage. It's absurd, Adam!"

"I don't think so."

Simon spoke even more firmly.

"Well, I *do*. But I'll tell you what. Go and see Mo. She can hardly have a rendezvous in the woods if you're with her, can she? I'll go back to the boys' dorm and keep an eye on Forrest. If he goes into the woods, I'll follow him. How's that?"

Adam saw that he had no choice.

"OK. I guess."

"And be *nice* to Mo. Don't clam up on her."

"If you say so."

Reluctantly, Adam left the theatre and walked up to the teachers' cottage.

The kitchen smelt of freshly baked bread. Mo let Adam in with an anxious smile.

"Adam! I wasn't sure you'd make it. Had a tough day?"

"Not really."

"I'd call it a tough day, if I'd gone through the mauling you got in School Council this morning. What's Forrest got against you?"

Adam hated teachers asking him personal stuff. He was silent. Mo spoke again.

"Forrest has his problems, but his bark's worse than his bite."

"I've already felt his bite, thank you very much."

Mo gave him what was probably meant to be a considerate smile.

"Mark told me about this morning. I doubt very much that Anthony would have actually struck you with the hot toaster."

"That wasn't what I was talking about."

"Oh."

Mo smiled sympathetically. Adam understood the technique. The teacher was silent for a while in the hope that he'd come up with a revelation. Well, it wasn't going to work on him. Eventually, Mo spoke again.

"Why'd you decide to come to this school, Adam?"

"Dunno."

"Most people come here for a fresh start. . . ."

"I guess."

Mo threw her hair back over her shoulders, exasperated. She raised her voice.

"You know, Adam, you act as though your dislike of school is unusual. It's not. One out of four students hate school – they probably have good reason to. One in three come from what used to be called 'broken homes' – that's not *unusual*, either. What is unusual is the huge chip on your shoulder."

She paused, still waiting for a reaction.

"Is it something to do with your father?"

Adam was silent. Mo spoke more firmly.

"It's not unusual to hate your father, Adam."

"I don't know him well enough to hate him."

Mo shook her head.

"Come on! You can *only* hate people who you don't really know. And you've got plenty of reasons to hate Simon. You've hardly seen him since you were three years old."

"How do you know that?"

Mo smiled.

"Teachers do talk about things other than education, you know. Simon's a nice man. But he feels guilty about neglecting you. He doesn't know how to talk to you. He thinks that his being a teacher may be part of the reason you're so disaffected with school."

"He may be right," Adam mumbled.

Mo looked at her watch.

"Yes. He might."

She appeared distracted. Adam thought that he knew why. "Look, Adam, I'm sorry. I didn't expect our conversation to go on for so long. I've arranged to meet another student in a few minutes. I think we've made some headway, don't you? Can we talk again next week?"

"Yeah. OK."

She offered him her hand. He shook it.

"Make the most of this place," Mo told him. "It has a lot to offer."

Adam walked slowly away from the teachers' cottage, looking for somewhere to hide. He needed to see if Mo went to meet Forrest in the woods. Mark Rhodes passed him on the path.

"You haven't seen Naomi, have you, Adam? I wanted to check that she's OK."

Adam shook his head. He couldn't tell Mark that Naomi was hiding in the woods.

"How do you find her at the moment?" Mark asked.

"I think she's coping pretty well."

Mark sighed.

"That's good. I rang her father with the news. She hadn't called him herself. He's very worried about her. Has she told you about her dad?"

"Not really," Adam said. "Only about her mother and how she died when Naomi was young."

"Did Naomi tell you exactly how her mother died?"

Adam thought for a moment.

"I guess . . . no. I got the impression that it was an accident, or something."

Mark furrowed his eyebrows. He seemed to be deciding whether to tell Adam something.

"You might as well know. Naomi finds it hard to talk about it. Her mother killed herself – shot herself, in fact – ten years ago. Obviously, that makes the way that Kate died even more painful to her."

"Yes. I can see that."

Mark went on. "I only found this out the other day. Kate told me, just before she died. Kate loved Naomi like a daughter. So, you see, she's lost two mothers now. This is a hard time for her."

Adam couldn't think of anything to say. Mark muttered good night and went into the cottage. Adam stood in the shadows of a large oak tree. A few moments after Mark had gone in, Mo came out. She began to walk, not towards the bridge, as Adam had expected, but down to the river bank, in the opposite direction. It would be easy for Naomi to miss her. Adam had to go after her.

Mo was easy to follow. She wore the same, light yellow dufflecoat as the previous night. Adam had only black jeans and a dark T-shirt on. It was chilly by the river, but at least he couldn't be seen easily. He watched the counsellor stumble along the river bank. Adam didn't understand where she was going. Then something mysterious happened. Mo seemed to float across the river and alight on the other side. A moment later, she vanished into the woods. What was going on? Not sure how far away Mo was, Adam crept up to the spot where she had crossed the river. There, he found an aluminium bridge, too low to be seen from the school grounds. Careful not to make a sound, he tiptoed across it. There was a rough path on the other side. Adam moved as quickly as he dared, listening out for the voices of Mo and Forrest. He was worried. If Mo came from an unexpected direction, she might surprise Naomi.

Somewhere ahead of him was the sound of branches being pushed aside. A black shape fluttered over Adam's head. Adam ducked, then looked up. It was only a bat. Next, Adam heard Mo's voice, clear in the still night.

"You!"

Then there was a gun-shot.

Adam froze. The woods seemed to come alive with bird and animal noises, full of panic. There was also a more human sounding, scuffling noise. Adam didn't know whether to go and investigate or to play safe, and run for help. Before he could decide, there was a second gun-shot, followed by a loud, human moan. More wildlife noises. Adam was scared out of his mind. It was too dangerous to get any closer. He heard footsteps, but couldn't tell whether they were coming towards or going away from him. He pressed himself against a large beech tree, hoping not to be seen.

Then there was a third shot. This time, the woods were completely silent. Then the screaming started.

"Naomi!"

Adam ran towards the sounds of her screams. Naomi stood in the clearing where Mo and Forrest had met the previous night. Her whole body was shaking. Adam held her, tightly.

"What happened? Tell me what happened!"

She pointed to the two bodies on the ground.

"I think they're both dead."

Adam looked at the bodies. One was Mo Highton. The other was Viscount Anthony Forrest.

"Who did it?" he asked her.

Naomi shook her head.

"I couldn't tell. I was too far away. I hadn't even

switched the tape recorder on. But I think whoever it was went over there."

She pointed in the direction of the path back to the school.

"We won't catch him now," Adam told her.

Naomi was still shaking. She found it hard to get the words out.

"I heard something," Naomi spluttered, urgently. "I think he fell."

Adam ran in the direction that she was pointing. The woods were dark and threatening, but he didn't have to look hard. On the other side of the clearing, a body lay on the ground. Adam had no trouble recognising the unconscious man with the gun by his side.

It was his father.

12

Naomi joined Adam on the edge of the clearing.

"Him," she said. "It was him all along. You must have known. That's why you helped me. I trusted you...."

Crying, she began to beat her fists against Adam's chest, hard. He felt ashamed: not because his father was a murderer, but because he, Adam, had told Simon about the meeting tonight. He had caused two innocent people to be killed.

"Why?" he said to Naomi. "I don't understand why he did it."

"You're lying," she told him. "I won't believe another word you say. You said you wouldn't come tonight, but you did. You must have known what kind of person your father was. You lied to me."

"I didn't. . . ."

Adam stopped. There was no point in arguing. She was right to blame him. They stood there, facing each other, tears running down Naomi's face. Then she left. Adam supposed that she would call the police, an ambulance. On the ground next to him, his father began to moan, softly. Adam felt like kicking him, but he knew it wouldn't help. Instead, he went back into the clearing.

Forrest's body was by the stump in the middle. He must have been sitting on it, waiting for Mo, when he heard Simon shooting the counsellor. Then Forrest would have got up, but not fast enough. The bullet had gone through his head, from close range. Mo Highton was about three metres from him, on the edge of the clearing. She had been shot in the chest. The deep red stain on the front of her dufflecoat was still spreading. It was hard for Adam to believe that he'd been talking to her only minutes ago. Adam thought that he saw one of Mo's eyelids flicker. He leant forward and listened for her breathing, but heard nothing. Just to be sure, Adam took Mo's wrist and felt for a pulse. In the distance he could hear the siren of an ambulance. At first he wasn't sure. But when the siren stopped, the pulse was still there: faint, but recognisable. Adam stood. Frantically, he ran back towards the school grounds, his heart pounding. At the end of the driveway, he could hear Phil Merchant asking the ambulance personnel just who had called them.

Adam got within shouting range as the first police car pulled up.

"Come quickly," he bellowed, as the whole school

started to pour out into the cool night air. "One of them's still alive!"

Adam guided the ambulance workers to the clearing where the bodies lay. Simon Lane sat on the edge of the clearing, with his head in his hands.

"What's happening?"

Adam ignored him.

"She's there. I thought I found a faint pulse."

Mo was carefully lifted onto a stretcher. As they carried the unconscious woman away, Simon Lane rose unsteadily to his feet. Two police officers approached from the path.

"There's a gun," Adam told them, "on the ground just by him."

"Adam."

Simon seemed to see his son for the first time.

"What happened?"

Again, Adam ignored his father. One of the police officers used a branch to pick up the gun and put it into an evidence bag. The other began to speak.

"You have the right to remain silent, but anything you do say may be taken down and used in evidence against you."

Adam watched as they handcuffed his father and led him away.

When Adam got back to the school grounds, Phil Merchant was ordering the last of the students back into their bedrooms. Mark Rhodes was helping.

"Where's Naomi?" Adam asked the English teacher.

"She's with Inspector Carter."

"It was her who called the police, then?"

"I think so." Mark looked upset and angry, in equal measures. "Now, will you please explain to me what you were doing in the woods?"

Adam explained about the conversation he'd overheard the previous night.

"It seems that I misinterpreted it."

Mark nodded.

"And you told your father?"

"Yes."

"And he realised that the game was up unless he killed them both?"

"I suppose, yes."

Mark shook his head slowly.

"At least you didn't tell him that Naomi was going to be there. Otherwise she'd be dead, too."

The police came for Adam. Mo was being taken to Airedale Hospital. Her condition was critical. Naomi, they told him, had been sedated.

"She was in shock," Inspector Carter told him, "so we couldn't get as much from her as we'd have liked. When you're ready, I want you to go over the sequence of events in the woods in as much detail as you can remember."

Adam did as he was told. The Inspector questioned him closely on the number of shots and the delay between them. Finally, she asked:

"Is there anything else that you can remember? Anything that might be remotely relevant?"

"Not that I can think of."

"You'll be questioned again tomorrow."

She paused, then added.

"You might be thinking about leaving this place. I could understand you wanting to get away after what's happened."

"I haven't really . . ."

"Don't. At least not until we tell you we're done with you. You're a material witness. I'm not sure how reliable the girl will be. We appreciate that you have feelings for your father. But don't leave. Understood?"

Adam understood that. It was everything else which had him completely confused. He went back to his room and lay down on the top bunk. Maybe he ought to call his mum. He hadn't spoken to her since he arrived. He'd been trying not to think about her. They'd been barely talking when he left. The Inspector was right. Eventually, he'd have to go home. What was the point in staying here after what had happened? Naomi hated him, and so would everyone else. Adam wanted nothing to do with his father, ever again. Nevertheless, a thought kept whirling around his head. Why? Maybe Simon had killed Forrest and Mo to protect himself, but why had he shot Kate Dance in the first place?

Adam couldn't sleep. Otherwise, he wouldn't have heard the boys whispering as they crept down the corridor at five in the morning. Adam got out of bed as quickly as he could and shoved the pillows from the bottom bunk under his duvet. Outside, a debate was going on.

"Just scare him?"

"Scare him? He's going to bleed!"

Adam opened his wardrobe and squeezed inside. The last thing he wanted was another beating. He had only just recovered from the one three nights before. His door opened. Three boys entered. From the part open door of the wardrobe, he saw the barrel of a familiar shotgun.

"Wake up, Lane!" a young voice shouted. "This is for Forrest!"

The boy fired twice into the duvet, then ran off.

When he was sure they weren't coming back, Adam got out of the wardrobe. He turned on the desk light and examined the pillows which he had substituted for his body. The pellets had pierced the duvet and lodged in the foam packing inside the pillow. They might have pierced Adam's skin, too – at that range, they could have hurt him badly. It was ironic, he thought – those were young kids, not Forrest's henchmen. And Adam had told them where to find the gun. He couldn't spend another night in the dorm. He dressed, opened the dorm door and walked out into the cold, moonlit night.

The police cars had gone. Over in the woods he could see the yellow tape that marked off the scene of the crime. A single light burned in the Grange – Phil Merchant's study. Perhaps the police were in there, or maybe Phil couldn't sleep, either. There was also a light on in the teachers' cottage. Mark Rhodes must be awake. Adam thought of going over to speak to him. He could certainly do with talking to someone. But before he could decide what to do, a voice hissed at him.

"Hey, son!"

It was a pale figure in jeans and a leather blouson.

"How'd you like to make some quick money?"

The man held out a card. It read "Press".

"Who got shot here last night?"

Adam stared back coldly at the man.

"You need to see the acting Headteacher, Mr Merchant."

"Come on!" The man gave Adam a pleading look. "I need to file by ten if I'm going to make the first editions of the evening papers. All I need is for you to confirm a few facts. There's fifty quid in it for you."

Adam started to walk away from him. The man reached into his pocket and held out five twenty-pound notes.

"I'll make it a hundred. Just tell me what you know – it doesn't matter how much. I'll keep it easy for you: just answer 'yes' or 'no'."

"No."

"Is the dead man Lord Forrest's son, Anthony?"

Adam was silent.

"Was he having an affair with the teacher who was shot?"

"She wasn't a teacher. She was a counsellor."

The man nodded and scribbled in his notebook.

"Have you any idea how long he'd been sleeping with her?"

"He wasn't . . ."

Adam shut up. He knew how these people worked. They twisted everything you said.

"I'm not telling you anything."

"The man who's been arrested – Simon Lane – was he also seeing this counsellor woman?"

Irritated, Adam snapped: "He'd only been at the school five days!"

"But they *were* living together, weren't they?"

"No! She was living in the same cottage as my father, that's all."

The reporter smiled.

"Your father, you say . . ."

A loud voice interrupted him.

"Who the hell are you?"

"Neil Andrew. I'm a freelance journalist. Are you Mr Merchant?"

"Yes. And you're in my school without permission. Get out!"

"You'll do much better if you talk to me. Just a few words. . . ."

Merchant shook his head.

"No comment. I'll issue a statement tomorrow."

"If you could just confirm or deny . . ."

"Get out!"

The journalist smiled apologetically and looked over Adam's shoulder.

"Chris! Over here!"

Adam and Phil turned round. A flash bulb went off in their faces. The photographer grinned. Neil Andrew slapped Adam on the back.

"Headteacher and murderer's son: the perfect picture! Thanks a lot, mate."

Phil Merchant made a growling noise.

"All right, all right. We're going."

As the two men sprinted up the hill, Phil Merchant turned to Adam.

"I'm sorry," Adam said. "They just turned up. I couldn't sleep. Some boys tried to . . ."

"You stupid, stupid fool!" Phil Merchant interrupted

him. "You and your father have ruined this school, do you know that? Ruined it! Just when we thought we'd turned the corner."

Adam didn't know what to say.

"How could you talk to those vermin?"

"I didn't . . ."

"Have you no shame? Get out of my sight. Go on, *get out!*"

Adam turned and walked off into the night. He wished that he could curl up in a ball and sleep for a long, long time. But he had nowhere left to go.

13

Adam woke at midday. He had slept behind the stage in the theatre, which his father had left unlocked the previous day. He'd found some smelly old blankets to wrap himself in, and had nodded off around dawn. Now, he left the theatre without washing, and walked towards the Grange, keeping his head down. He knew how unpopular he must be today, but there was nowhere else for him to go. As he passed groups of students, they turned away. Some hissed and directed loud obscenities at him. Adam felt sick. He had become a pariah.

The police had the lane leading to the school blocked off, but, as Adam approached the Grange, they let a car through. Mark Rhodes got out of his beat-up old Morris Minor Traveller, a pile of newspapers under his arm. He waved to Adam.

"You look like you spent the night in a barn."

"Close."

Mark put his arm round Adam's shoulders.

"You're not very popular after last night. Have you phoned your mother yet?"

"I've only just woken up."

"Do it soon, before she reads it in the papers. Here, you'd better see these. Phil sent me to Halifax for them."

He held out the bundle of first editions of the evening papers. Adam scanned the headlines: SCHOOL OF SHAME!, BIZARRE LOVE TRIANGLE!, TEACHER SHOOTS TEENAGE VISCOUNT AND TWO TIMING LOVER, and, finally, in the *Sheffield Star*, SHOOT THE TEACHER! All of the stories were accompanied by photos of Lord Forrest and his family, together with the one of Phil Merchant and Adam looking dazed.

"The story's the same in all of them."

Adam read the "exclusive account by our own reporter, Neil Andrew".

> Mystery surrounds the exact circumstances of last night's shootings. Police refuse to say if the arrested man, Simon Lane, 39, is also being charged with the murder of Headteacher, Kate Dance, who was shot at her desk four days ago. Local residents are already linking the deaths with previous sex scandals at the school. "They should have closed it down two years ago," said Hebblethwaite vicar, Frank Norris.
>
> Acting Headteacher, Philip Merchant would give no comment last night, but the arrested man's son, Adam, a pupil at the school, spoke to me at length . . .

" 'At length'," Adam said. "I hardly told him anything!"

"I'm afraid it gets worse," Mark told him.

> *"I blame Beechwood school for this tragedy," Adam said. "Dad couldn't cope with the school's whole 'free love' thing. My father is a jealous man. Although he'd only been at the school for five days, he was passionately in love with Mo Highton. When he found out that she was seeing Viscount Anthony as well, he flipped, especially since Tony was only sixteen. I believe that he followed the couple into the woods and shot them while they were making love."*

"This is complete garbage!" Adam said. "I didn't say any of this. Can't I do something about it?"

"Was there anyone with you?"

"Not for most of the time. Phil arrived later, but . . ."

"Then it's your word against Andrew's, and the photographer. I'm afraid that's what they do, Adam. They make things up."

He took back the papers.

"I'd better take these up to Phil. I'd stay out of his way if I were you."

Adam sighed. "Trouble is, I need somewhere to sleep. I can't stay in the dorm. Three young kids tried to wound me with Forrest's shotgun last night."

Mark thought for a moment. "I'll tell you what. When the police have finished in the cottage, you can have Simon's room. I don't see how anyone can object to that."

"Thanks," Adam said. "You're a friend."

* * *

He went back to the dorm which, luckily, was quiet, and opened the door to his room. It had been totally trashed. Torn clothes lay all over the place. Adam's CD player lay in pieces on the floor. Ugly graffiti was scrawled across his posters and the walls. The only thing they hadn't touched was the school work on his desk.

Adam quickly sorted out his belongings before anyone could come and cause more trouble. Nothing had been stolen. His wallet and his change pouch were where he had left them, in a drawer. He dug through his clothes and managed to find a T-shirt, a sweater and two changes of underwear that the vandals hadn't got to. Then he put them into his sports bag, together with his history project and a pair of headphones, which they'd missed.

There was a phone booth in the Grange's entrance hall. Adam rang his mum's work number. Would she have him back? He didn't know. The assistant manager answered.

"I'm sorry, Adam. Your mother's on holiday for a fortnight. I think she's gone to Spain with her boyfriend. Didn't she tell you?"

"Never mind."

Adam hung up. He'd forgotten his mum's holiday, which had been planned for months. So he was stuck at the Grange School for another ten days at least. He would have to make the best of it. As he was standing in the hall, Phil Merchant came down the stairs from his study.

"Ah, Adam. The Inspector wants to see you. She's in Kate's old room."

"OK."

They passed on the stairs. Phil signalled Adam to stop.

"Mark tells me you've seen the papers."

"Yes."

"I'm going on television in half an hour to say that the stories are a complete fiction. Promise me you won't say anything to contradict that."

"I won't say anything at all to anyone," Adam told him.

"Also, Lord Forrest is on his way down. He'll want to talk to you."

"OK."

"Try to avoid repeating the tales you've been telling about his son. There's no point in speaking ill of the dead."

Merchant didn't ask Adam how he was. He was only bothered about placating the peer. Adam didn't feel sorry that Forrest was dead. But he was sorry about the way the boy had died, and his part in it.

The Inspector was on the phone when Adam knocked on the door. She waved Adam to the chair where he had first sat four days before. There was no trace of the blood which had so recently covered Kate Dance's desk and carpet. The only other change was on the wall, where the timetable was. It had been replaced by a large diagram of the Grange School and the woods. Inspector Carter finished her phone call.

"Adam. I thought you ought to know that your father has been charged with the murders of Kate Dance and Anthony Forrest, together with the attempted murder of Maureen Highton. The last charge will also become murder if the victim doesn't survive."

"Why have you charged him with killing Kate?" Adam wanted to know.

"Tests show that the gun used last night was the same as the one used to kill Kate Dance."

"Oh."

"Did you know that your father had an unlicensed gun?"

"No."

"We've established that it was one of a pair of revolvers, bought two years ago in San Francisco. The name used to buy it was an obvious alias. Has your father visited America recently?"

Adam remembered a postcard, a baseball cap sent for his birthday, two sizes too small.

"Yes. At around that time."

Inspector Carter gave a small smile. She continued.

"Presumably, your father managed to evade the metal detector and smuggled both revolvers back to Britain. We're concerned that we haven't yet located the second gun. Any idea where it might be?"

"None."

The Inspector leant forward.

"We think that your father's motive in shooting the two people last night was to silence them. Our theory is that Viscount Forrest, while he was hiding in the school just before term started, saw or heard something which made him suspect that your father killed Kate Dance. Forrest then decided to confide in Maureen Highton, since she was the school counsellor. They met in secret, so that your father wouldn't stumble onto their conversation. But you gave the game away and your father realised that he had to kill them both."

She added, "Do you follow me so far?"

"Yes," said Adam. "But I'm not sure I agree with you. Why did Forrest go to Mo Highton? I thought that he was blackmailing her. If he wasn't, why didn't he just go to you?"

The Inspector gave him a condescending look.

"I've already gathered that you didn't like the Viscount. I can't say I was too impressed with him myself. But he wasn't all bad. It could be that, thanks to problems he'd had in the past, Viscount Forrest had good reasons not to trust the police. We think that's why he spoke to Ms Highton."

Adam still wasn't convinced.

"No," said the Inspector, "the real question is, then – *why* did your father kill Kate Dance? Do you have any thoughts on this?"

Adam shook his head vigorously.

"None at all."

"Do you have any idea why he resigned from his old job, to take one at half the salary? Was there, perhaps, some kind of scandal?"

Adam shook his head.

"I really don't know. Simon's virtually a stranger to me."

Inspector Carter nodded.

"I ought to tell you that your father is protesting his innocence."

Adam shrugged.

"Well he would, wouldn't he?"

"He's been asking to see you."

"Tough."

The Inspector adopted a friendlier tone.

"We'd very much appreciate it if you *would* visit him in prison. We'd like you to ask him why he killed Kate Dance."

Adam shrugged.

"I'd like to know the answer to that. But I've got no intention of seeing Simon ever again."

Inspector Carter leant forward and gave him a beseeching look.

"Don't do it for your father. Do it for us. To help the investigation."

She had Adam where she wanted him. He felt guilty about his part in the shootings last night. And he *did* want to understand Simon's motive.

"All right. I'll go this afternoon."

Carter offered Adam her hand.

"I'll get one of my officers to drive you."

As Adam was leaving, the Inspector asked a final question.

"You said that you heard three shots last night. Could you have been mistaken about the third one?"

"No. Definitely not."

"Odd," the Inspector said.

"Why?"

"We only recovered two bullets."

Adam left the office feeling like Judas. Simon may be guilty, but he was still Adam's father. Should Adam be helping the police to find out why he killed Kate? Who knew what went on between men and women, what terrible circumstance caused Simon to kill Kate Dance?

Adam wasn't sure that he'd understand even if his father told him. But he'd agreed to go now.

A group of girls were playing some kind of chase game just outside the Grange. Funny how quickly some people can get over death, Adam observed. Then they saw him. Immediately, the game ended. Four of the girls hissed. Two of them spat at him. Adam wanted to shout. "Don't blame me! It was my father!" But he knew there was no point. Thérèse Depigny, the languages teacher, came up behind him.

"You girls, you should be ashamed of yourselves! Go to your rooms."

They scuttled off. The teacher turned to Adam.

"Are you all right?"

He shrugged.

"Everyone blames me for what my father did."

Thérèse Depigny nodded.

" 'Though guiltless, you shall expiate your father's sins'."

"What does 'expiate' mean?"

"Atone for, or pay the penalty. It comes from a Latin poet, Horace."

She looked at his bag.

"Going somewhere?"

He explained that the bag held all the stuff he had left.

"Perhaps it would be best if you left here."

"The police won't let me."

Another group of children walked by, each of them giving Adam the evil eye. The teacher shrugged.

"Adolescents can be the cruellest people in the world. They are the least tolerant of all groups. One day, perhaps, they will be ashamed of the way they are behaving now. But that is of little comfort to you today."

She patted Adam on the back.

"Come on! It's time you had your first languages lesson. We'll go to the lab and see how much you remember."

For the next hour, Adam was immersed in vocabulary and verb constructions. The teacher constantly prodded him to concentrate harder. The work was a merciful release from the tension of the last few days. Time seemed to vanish. Then, just when Adam thought that he was beginning to get somewhere, the police came to take him to his father.

Simon had bags under his eyes and hadn't shaved. His hair hung limply, failing to conceal his bald patch. When Adam arrived, he tried to make light of his surroundings.

"They keep asking me why I resigned from my old job, as though it might explain the murders. I feel like Patrick McGoohan in *The Prisoner*. Remember: 'Just tell us one thing, number six, why did you resign?'"

He smiled feebly.

"Although they haven't given me a number yet."

"Why *did* you resign?" Adam asked.

Simon shrugged.

"As I keep telling them, it was for really mundane reasons – I didn't enjoy the job any more. The government were turning the clock back twenty years and I had to implement the changes. I hated it. Every departmental meeting I was giving out bad news – endless exams and assessments that were nothing to do with education. So I quit.

"That was all there was to it – no scandal, no smoking gun, just another teacher who'd had enough. But I had an escape clause. Kate had been in touch a couple of times to try to persuade me to come and work with her. She said we'd have the opportunity to put into practice the ideals we'd had when we were teaching students together."

He paused, then added.

"But we never got the chance."

Simon's tone was convincing, but Adam didn't know whether he believed him or not. Simon tried to make conversation.

"So how're you getting on at school? Finished your history project yet?"

"Not quite."

"I'm beginning to have a lot of sympathy for Dreyfus," Simon said. "He was framed, too, you know. Transported for life to Devil's Island. But then the bloke who set him up confessed. He killed himself and Dreyfus was given a pardon. Eventually, he was totally cleared. He went on to fight in the First World War – survived that, too. So there's hope for me yet!"

Adam tried to laugh. His father's eyes were red. His voice turned hoarse.

"I didn't do it, Adam. I didn't kill anybody!"

Adam wanted to get out of the claustrophobic interview room. All he had to do was get up and leave. He owed Simon Lane nothing. The only thing they shared, as far as Adam was concerned, was their second name. And he would rather not have had that.

He would rather have kept his mother's name, like Naomi.

"I'm sorry, Simon. I don't believe you."

Simon slumped forward. Adam thought that he was about to cry. Instead, he began to speak again, in an insistent voice.

"Since they left me alone, I've been trying to work out what happened. Who killed Kate, and why, who framed me for the other murders."

"Framed you?"

"Yes. Somebody shot Forrest and Mo, then shot at me as I was trying to get away from the carnage. They missed, but I cracked my head against a tree when I fell to the floor. While I was unconscious, they planted the gun on me. Whoever it was must have actually put the gun in my hand, because it had my fingerprints on it."

Adam shook his head. The story was too incredible. Simon went on. "They even claim that I stole the key to Kate's office and had a copy made — oh, yes, someone did. Someone had a key of that type made in Hebden Bridge, the day I went in to have the Escort's window replaced. Unfortunately, no-one in the hardware store can remember what the person looked like. So they've got me again."

Simon was rambling, Adam thought. He went on.

"The third bullet. The third bullet would prove it. The police say that it doesn't exist, that no-one fired at me, that I knocked myself out as I was running away. But that's even more ridiculous."

Adam stood up to go.

"Why did you kill Kate?" he asked.

"I didn't kill her," Simon said. "She was the only woman I ever really loved."

Adam turned to face his father again, not believing what he'd heard.

"Pardon?"

Simon spoke slowly and quietly.

"Kate and I were lovers, fourteen years ago. It was when we were on the teacher training course. At the end of the year, I left you and your mother and moved in with Kate. We lived together for a year when the course was over, both teaching in London.

"But I'd fallen for her more heavily than she'd fallen for me – or maybe it was that education was always more important to her than anything else – Kate left me to do voluntary service in Africa. We never got together again after that, but we stayed in touch. That's how she came to offer me the job at the Grange."

Adam shook his head with disbelief. His mother had never even told him that Simon left for another woman – he'd thought that they were incompatible, or that Simon wasn't ready for kids – but Kate ... for a moment Adam found himself imagining what it would have been like to have her as his stepmother. Then he began to get angry.

"Why didn't you tell me about Kate before?"

"Because you wouldn't have given her a chance. Kate is ... was, a fine woman. I wanted you to like her."

"I'm sorry, Simon. I don't know what to think."

"Come and see me again. Help me to clear myself."

"I don't know," Adam said again. "Maybe."

* * *

"Well," said Inspector Carter, outside the room. "Did he tell you anything useful?"

Adam felt torn in two. He didn't know what to believe any more. The police, he was sure, would find out about Simon's relationship with Kate sooner or later. But he couldn't be the one to tell them.

"No," he said, decisively. "Nothing at all."

14

Adam was lost in the woods. Somewhere, not far away, he could hear Naomi screaming. Somebody was trying to hurt her, but Adam couldn't make out where she was. He stumbled into a clearing with a large oak stump in the middle of it. Slowly, a body rose from behind the stump. It was Forrest. The middle of the boy's head was missing, but his eyes were still in place and they were filled with hatred. Forrest cocked his shotgun and pointed it at Adam. Adam ducked. There was a scream from behind him. He looked back. Mo Highton had fallen to the ground. Blood poured from her chest.

"This can't be happening!" Adam shouted.

Then his father stepped into the clearing. He held a revolver. Somewhere behind him, Adam could hear Naomi complain, "Get Adam out of here. Get Adam out!" Simon held the revolver by its barrel and handed it to Adam.

"Here. Why don't you finish what you started?"

Adam took the gun and pointed it at his father. Forrest stood to the left of Simon, laughing. Adam shifted the gun, pointing it at Forrest instead. But before Adam could shoot, he watched in horror as the boy's head split in two. Slowly, the rest of Forrest's body divided itself down the middle and each half slithered to the ground. Only the laughing remained.

Adam pointed the revolver at his father. He pressed his finger on the trigger. But before he could fire, there was another gun-shot. Adam's father fell to the floor, dead. Someone was walking towards Adam, out of the shadowy woods. He couldn't see who it was, but he could see that the person was holding a revolver identical to his.

"I want him out, now!"

"Naomi, calm down!"

And then Adam was awake, in his father's bed. He could hear Naomi arguing with Mark Rhodes.

"He betrayed me!"

Mark replied calmly.

"No, he didn't. You're being melodramatic, as usual. Adam had no way of knowing that his father was the killer. I still find it hard to believe myself. I've told him that he can stay here until he leaves the school, which will only be a day or two longer, I suspect."

Naomi remained agitated.

"I can't sleep under the same roof as him!"

Mark continued to speak in a calming voice.

"It's really about time you moved back to the dorm,

anyway. At the moment, Adam needs to stay here more than you do. He isn't safe anywhere else."

"I hate you!"

Adam heard Naomi slamming the door. A minute later, Mark knocked on Adam's door. He came in holding a mug of tea.

"I was afraid that row would have woken you up. You mustn't mind Naomi. She's under a lot of stress at the moment."

Adam drank his tea.

"Will you go to lessons today?" Mark asked.

"Maybe."

"It'll do you good. Keep your mind off things."

"OK. I'll try."

After Mark had left, Adam showered and dressed. Then he walked to the Grange. His mind was still turning over what Simon had told him yesterday. If Simon were guilty, why would he tell Adam about his affair with Kate? On the other hand, suppose the affair didn't end thirteen years ago, but had carried on. Suppose Kate and Simon had quarrelled?

"Ah, here he is."

Phil Merchant was standing next to a fierce-looking man in a tweed coat. Adam recognised the portly figure from his photograph in the papers. Lord Forrest.

"I was looking for you in the dorm," Phil said. "Lord Forrest would like a word with you."

Phil had an odd expression in his eyes. Presumably he had seen the carnage that was once Adam's room.

"And when you're finished, I'd like you to come to my study, please."

Adam exchanged an awkward hello with the dead boy's father.

"Let's go for a walk," the peer said.

Lord Forrest and Adam walked side by side towards the woods.

"I want to know why my son died," the peer told Adam. "The police say one thing, the papers another. But you were there. What do you say?"

"I haven't seen this morning's papers," Adam told him. "But the 'interview' they printed yesterday was all lies. I didn't say a word of it – I expect Phil told you that."

"Yes."

"So I guess Forre – your son saw something, the night of Kate's murder, which incriminated my father."

Lord Forrest shook his head.

"But that's impossible. My son was on the train to Edinburgh at the time of her death. My wife met him off the train."

Adam shrugged.

"Maybe he heard something which indicated that my dad was going to kill her. I really don't know. I don't know why my father killed Kate Dance."

The peer gave Adam a searching look.

"You hated Anthony, didn't you?"

Adam stalled.

"Why do you say that?"

"It was you who reported his presence in the school during the holidays. He attacked you on the morning before he was murdered. It's recorded in the school log book."

"We were enemies. Yes."

They were in the woods now, on the edge of the clearing where it had all happened. The yellow police tape was gone. They stopped walking. Lord Forrest turned to Adam.

"My son was a disturbed boy. This was the only school we found which was able to contain him. He could be ... cruel. But that doesn't mean his life deserved to end the way it did. I need to know why he died – who killed him, and what their motive was. So far, the facts don't add up."

"No," Adam agreed. "They don't."

"I'm trained as a lawyer," Lord Forrest boasted. "I can think of one person other than your father who had both the motive and the opportunity to kill my son."

Adam was silent. He could tell what was coming. The peer cleared his throat.

"Did you kill him, Adam?"

Before Adam could answer, Naomi appeared, wearing black jeans and a black T-shirt. She was coming from the direction of the clearing.

"I've been listening to your conversation," she said. "Adam didn't kill your son. You might as well accuse me of doing it. Adam was further away from the scene than I was."

Adam told Lord Forrest who she was.

"What do you think you're doing here?" the peer asked.

Naomi replied calmly.

"Inspector Carter asked me to look at the scene of the crime again, to see if I could remember anything I'd missed the other night. I could hardly avoid overhearing your conversation."

Lord Forrest harrumphed.

"If there's nothing else either of you have to tell me...."

"There isn't," Adam said.

Naomi remained quiet. The large man stomped back in the direction of the school. Adam and Naomi faced each other.

"Thanks for getting me out of that," Adam told her.

Naomi shrugged.

"I hate people like him," she said. "They think that because they own everything, they know everything...."

Her voice tailed off. Then she added.

"Don't think I've forgiven you. You could have got me killed the other night."

"I'm sorry," Adam said. "I had no idea...."

Naomi stared at the ground.

"I don't suppose you did."

Anxious to gain her confidence, Adam told her about his conversation with Simon, including the revelation that his father had had an affair with Naomi's aunt.

"Anyway," he added at the end, "when Mo recovers consciousness, she'll be able to tell us who did it, won't she?"

Naomi didn't look convinced.

"Maybe," Naomi said. "Presuming she does recover. But shock often affects people's memories. I wouldn't bet on it."

"Can we be friends again?" Adam asked her. "You're about the only one I've got here – well, you and Mark."

Naomi smiled assent. Clumsily, Adam put his arm

around her waist. They exchanged an awkward embrace.

"Let's go back," she said, as they pulled apart.

"No, wait a minute."

Adam led Naomi back into the clearing.

"My dad said that the police haven't found the third bullet – the one which he says was fired at him. I just want a quick look around."

"They mentioned that to me, too," Naomi said. "But I only heard two shots."

Adam examined the area around the tree where he had found his father. Naomi helped him.

"Do you *really* think your father might be innocent?"

"I don't know. I'd like some proof. Like Lord Forrest said, there's a lot of things that don't add up. You didn't actually see him shooting, did you?"

Naomi shook her head.

"It all happened so fast. I was scared that whoever it was would see me there, too. None of it's very clear."

Adam looked around. He could find nothing near the tree and, anyway, the police were bound to have searched this part of the woods thoroughly. He walked to the middle of the clearing. The oak stump was still stained with some of Forrest's blood. Uneasily, Adam remembered the dream which had woken him that morning.

"Listen," he said to Naomi. "Forrest and Mo were both shot from close range. Let's assume for a moment that my father was telling the truth – that someone shot at him, too. He ducked, and banged his head, knocking himself out. The person who shot at him would be standing somewhere around here."

Naomi nodded.

"Therefore, the bullet would have landed somewhere over there." He pointed towards a dense patch of trees thirty metres away.

"Want to help me look?"

For the next hour, the two spread out and carefully examined the whole area, looking for the spent bullet which could exonerate Simon Lane. By the time the hour was up, Adam was beginning to doubt that the third shot had ever been fired. After all, Naomi, who was closer to the shooting, couldn't remember it.

"Come on," he said to her. "Let's forget it."

He was walking past an area they had already covered. Suddenly, Adam noticed a sign they'd missed earlier."

"Look."

There was a round hole in the bark of the tree. The bark had been pulled away so that you could see how far the bullet had penetrated: nearly two inches. But the bullet wasn't there any longer. Adam called Naomi.

"Someone's been here before us."

She examined the bark.

"You're right. But who?"

"It couldn't have been my father. He's in prison."

"I doubt that it'd be any of the kids from school," Naomi said. "Phil announced yesterday that the woods were out of bounds until further notice."

They walked back towards the school. Adam tried to make some sense out of his latest discovery.

"Suppose," he said, "there was someone else here – someone who Forrest recognised, and connected with Kate's killing."

"In that case," Naomi said, "it could have been anyone – a stranger, a psychopath. . . ."

"Not anyone," Adam replied. "Just before the first shot, I heard Mo say 'you'. She recognised whoever shot her."

"Maybe," Naomi said. "It's beginning to sound like there were a lot of people in the woods last night."

"Adam!"

It was Phil Merchant, calling from the window of his office.

"You were meant to come and see me an hour ago."

"I think I'll drive to Airedale Hospital," Naomi said, "see how Mo is." As Naomi got into Kate's car, Adam climbed the stairs to Phil's office. The acting Headteacher motioned him to sit down.

"Kate's funeral has been set for tomorrow."

"What did the coroner's court say?" Adam asked.

"Unlawful killing by person or persons unknown. However, the police seem convinced that your father is guilty."

Adam said nothing. Phil went on.

"They also say that they have no further need to question you. Therefore, I'm going to have to ask you to leave the school by this evening. I'm sure you don't need telling that your presence here is an embarrassing and painful reminder of recent events. I want you gone before the funeral."

"I want to go to it."

"I don't think that's advisable. The family wouldn't like it."

Adam became angry.

"The only 'family' that I know of is Naomi. I'm sure she wouldn't object."

Now Merchant raised his voice. "I can't stop you attending this funeral, Adam. But I can ask you to leave this school. I want you gone by the end of the afternoon."

Adam wasn't having it. "I don't have anywhere to go. My mother's on holiday. Simon's in gaol. Anyway, I thought this school didn't expel students."

"We don't, and I don't want to set a precedent. Remember, you were accepted as a non-fee paying student. That was not because you were a deserving case, but because your father worked here. Those circumstances no longer apply. However, if you choose not to leave, a School Council meeting can be called. You know from the meeting two days ago that most students want you out."

Adam stood up. "I'm not going until I know exactly what happened," he said. "Then you won't see me for dust."

He turned his back on Phil.

"My decision stands," Merchant called, as Adam closed the door behind him. "I want you out by the end of the afternoon."

15

After leaving Merchant, Adam didn't know where to go. The quietest place he could think of was the library, so he found himself a study cubicle and hid in there, where nobody was likely to find him. He needed time to think. But it didn't work. Five minutes later, he heard a familiar voice.

"He might be here."

It was Tanya. She was with Matthew.

"We were looking for you," Matthew told him. "I went to get you to do breakfast this morning and saw what they'd done to your room."

"That hardly matters now," Adam told them. "Merchant's given me until the end of this afternoon to get out of the school."

"He can't do that!"

Tanya sounded indignant.

"He just did."

Matthew thought aloud.

"The School Council . . ."

Adam interrupted.

"Would support Merchant, if we called a meeting. . . ."

Tanya seemed upset.

"It's not fair – your dad's the guilty one, not you. . . ."

Adam shook his head.

"I'm not even certain that he is guilty, though the police seem sure he is. I think that someone might have set Simon up. Whoever it was must be in the school now."

"Then you can't leave," Matthew said. "You'll have to hide out until you find out who did it."

"I know." Adam frowned. "But Naomi's out of school right now, and I can't do it alone."

"You don't need Naomi," Tanya told him. "Matthew and I'll help you."

Two hours later, Mark Rhodes drove Adam to Hebblethwaite station. He bought Adam his ticket to London.

"You're sure that you'll find someone to put you up?"

Adam nodded.

"Don't see me off. I'd like to be on my own for a while."

Mark offered Adam his hand.

"I'm sorry that it's all worked out like this."

When the English teacher had gone, Adam walked back to the Grange the way Naomi had shown him –

over the crags, through the fields and woods, then back into school by darkness. This took an hour-and-a-half. Tanya was waiting for him in the theatre.

"I saved you some food."

Adam ate the cold, stodgy stew hungrily.

"Your friend Naomi's back. But she went straight round to the teachers' cottage, so I haven't been able to tell her that you're still here."

Adam was annoyed. He didn't want Naomi to believe he'd deserted her. She would think that he hadn't even left a goodbye message.

"What's Matthew doing?" Adam asked her.

"He was going to hang around the Grange. The police are still there. He thought he might find something out."

Tanya sat down. For the first time, Adam noticed the T-shirt she was wearing. It read "We Didn't Start The Fire". He laughed.

"What's so funny?"

He pointed. Tanya looked annoyed.

"Oh that. It was a friend's idea of a joke after I torched the science block at my secondary school."

"You're not planning to burn down the Grange, too?"

"Nah. Everything's made of stone. Wouldn't burn well." She smiled. "I'll tell you what, though. . . ."

"What?"

"If all the rumours that are going round are true, and the school gets closed down, I think I'll torch the new teaching block. It's really ugly, and it'd go like a catherine wheel."

Adam couldn't tell if she was being serious or joking.

"Do you hate school that much?"

Tanya shrugged.

"Some of it. I like music, playing with keyboards, that sort of thing. I hated English before I came here, but Mark Rhodes is all right. I even went to one of your dad's sessions. He was pretty good, too – didn't seem like a murderer to me."

"I don't know," Adam said. "What does a murderer look like?"

"Like you, according to the latest reports," said a voice from behind them. Tanya and Adam jumped. Matthew had come in while they were absorbed in their conversation.

"*What?*"

Matthew sat down.

"I've just been listening outside Phil Merchant's door. Inspector Carter was furious with Phil for sending you home without telling her first. She gave him a real going over. Evidently, some new information's emerged, about your dad and Kate Dance. They think that *you* might have killed Kate – something about revenge for you and your mother – then killed Forrest because he got in the way, and framed your dad for both killings!"

"That's ridiculous," Tanya said.

"No, it's not," Adam told her. "It makes perfect sense. Dad must have told them about his affair with Kate, and that I knew about it. So they decided he didn't have a motive, but I did. Have they let him go?"

"No," Matthew said. "They won't until Mo gets out of her coma or you're found. When you didn't show up at St Pancras, they sent loads of police to comb the stations at Leeds, Sheffield, Chesterfield . . . anywhere you might have changed trains or got off in between."

Tanya laughed.

"You were lucky that Phil booted you out when he did!"

Matthew shook his head.

"It won't take them long to work out that you never left. And there aren't too many places to hide in the school. We need to find who the real killer is, and quickly."

They spent the next hour going over all the events of the last few days. None of it seemed any clearer to Adam. However, Tanya and Matthew were seeing some of the facts with a fresh eye. Maybe it would help. When they'd exhausted all the details, Matthew was silent. After five minutes, he said: "The police are right. The most logical suspect is you, Adam. But there *are* flaws in their argument — where did you get the guns from? And how did you find out about your father and Kate Dance before he told you? The second most obvious suspect is your father. He had the opportunity, but no motive. However, there's one suspect who hasn't been considered at all."

"Who's that?" both of them asked.

"A person who could easily have had a duplicate key cut and who Mo Highton would have recognised in the woods. The person who was passed over for the Headship, but got it when Kate died. The person who told everyone to stay out of the woods so that *he'd* have time to recover the third bullet. And the person who threw Adam out of the school before he could uncover the real culprit. The one person who's been above suspicion so far. . . ."

They looked at each other, then hissed the name out loud at the same time:

"Phil Merchant!"

16

Adam was woken by a sound like an amplified electric lawnmower above his head. It took him a moment to remember where he was: sleeping rough by the side of the stage in the theatre. He was unlikely to be disturbed today, since school was closed because of the funeral.

Adam got to the narrow window just in time to see the cause of the noise – a Lockheed helicopter, descending onto the school playing field. Landing complete, its rotor blades slowly ground to a halt. The craft was too far away for Adam to see who got out. There was a sink in the backstage area. Adam splashed himself with water and checked his watch. Just gone nine. The funeral was at three. Adam wanted to attend it, but, if he did, he was liable to get caught, even if he stayed in the background. Whatever happened, he had to talk to

Naomi. If he could tell her the Phil Merchant theory, it wouldn't matter so much if he was arrested.

The theatre door opened. Adam pressed his body against the wall, hoping he wouldn't be discovered. But it was Matthew. He had brought Adam a sandwich and a pint of milk.

"I've just seen Tanya. She says she heard Naomi come back to her room a few minutes ago. I don't know where she's been."

He looked out of the window.

"If you want to go outside without being noticed, now's a good time. Everyone's engrossed by that huge helicopter."

"Whose is it?"

"Dunno. The police maybe. The whole school's over there. I even saw Merchant going. Tanya's keeping an eye on them."

"OK."

Adam ate the sandwich quickly and left half the milk unfinished. When Matthew had double checked that the coast was clear, he walked as casually as he could over to the girls' dorm. There was still a police car by the Grange, Adam noticed. But Kate Dance's green 2CV was gone.

As he'd hoped, the building was deserted. Adam quickly made his way to Naomi's room. He opened the door without knocking.

"Naomi? Tanya told me you were . . ."

But the person in the room wasn't Naomi. It was Mark Rhodes. The English teacher was sat at Naomi's desk. By his left hand was a slightly squashed bullet.

"You!" Adam said. "It was you all along!"

Rhodes stood up. In his right hand was a revolver, exactly the same as the one that had been planted on Simon three nights before. Mark spoke. "Adam, this isn't what it . . ."

Adam didn't stay to hear the rest. He backed out of the room before Rhodes could shoot at him, and hurtled down the corridor out of the dorm. Behind him, Rhodes was silent.

"What the . . ."

Adam almost knocked Matthew over.

"Rhodes! It wasn't Merchant. It was Mark Rhodes all along. He was waiting for Naomi with a gun in his hand. He was the one who took the bullet from the tree!"

Matthew followed Adam towards the Grange.

"What are you going to do?"

"*You're* going to call the police. I've got to warn Naomi."

Matthew went into the school building to use the phone. Adam looked around. He no longer cared if he was spotted. After all, he was innocent. Somebody must know where Naomi was. He looked over towards the helicopter in the field. The students were coming away from it. Whoever was on it must have got out, left. Behind him, he heard another engine.

"Adam!"

It was Naomi, driving Kate's 2CV. She pulled up next to him.

"Christ, Naomi, where have you been? I've been going out of my . . ."

"I thought you'd left," Naomi interrupted him. "I've just been to the hospital again to see how Mo was.

She's still in a coma. Anyway, what are you doing here? The police said they were looking for you."

"You've got to get away," Adam told her. "You're in danger!"

Naomi was annoyed.

"You're the one in trouble, according to the police. . . ."

"Never mind that now," Adam told her, urgently. "Get inside the Grange. I'll explain there. It's really important, I promise."

Naomi became angry.

"Don't tell me what to do, Adam. No-one tells me what to do!"

Adam tried to calm himself down. Naomi had a quick temper, but he didn't have time to argue with her now.

"I think we should go into the Grange and wait for the police," he told Naomi. "There's something I need to warn you about."

"It'll have to wait," Naomi told him. "I need to have a shower and get changed for Kate's funeral. I'll see you there."

She started to walk away from Adam.

"You can't go back to your room," Adam told her. "I've just come from there. Mark Rhodes is waiting for you."

Naomi didn't seem perturbed.

"I'd better go and see him, then."

Adam began to shout.

"You don't understand – it's been him all along! Naomi, he's waiting for you with a gun!"

Naomi's face went white. Adam was sure that she

was going to faint. But then she turned round and continued walking towards the dorm.

"Where are you going?"

"I'm going to see Mark. I need to sort everything out."

"You need to what? Naomi, he might kill you."

"I'm going to see Mark."

Adam chased after her. He grabbed Naomi's shoulder. Naomi turned round and pushed him away with her fist. The punch hurt. She was stronger than she looked.

"You stupid, stupid jerk! You know nothing about Mark. Leave me alone!"

Adam still followed her.

"I won't let you get yourself killed!"

Naomi was inside the girls' dorm now. Adam followed her from a few paces behind. It was agony. She had come so close to getting killed the other night. Now she was walking straight into the murderer's trap. Adam's heart sank as she opened her bedroom door.

"Mark?"

Thankfully, there was no reply. Adam heard a rustle of papers as Naomi searched for something in her desk. Then she came out again.

"He's not here. He must have gone to the cottage."

"Leave him there," Adam told her. "Let the police get him."

"I need to talk to him!"

"I won't let you!"

Adam stood in front of the door to the dorm, blocking Naomi's exit.

"You won't get past me," he told her.

Naomi could see that he was right. If she wanted to get out, she would have to fight him, or go back and find a window that she could climb through. Naomi stared at Adam. It was an icy, frightening stare.

"Listen," she said. "You think that Mark shot Mo and Forrest?"

"Yes."

"But you told me yourself that you saw Mark go into the cottage that night, just before Mo left. Perhaps you'd like to explain how he managed to leave the cottage again, overtake you without your noticing, and shoot two people before you'd had time to get to the clearing?"

Adam was silenced. She was right, he realised. Mark couldn't have done it.

"But in that case, what was he . . .?"

Naomi interrupted him.

"You're thick, Adam Lane. Always have been, always will be. Now, will you let me pass?"

Adam got out of her way. Naomi marched by him, out of the dorm, onto the path which led to the teachers' cottage. Adam followed, still only a few paces behind. Dozens of students were making their way back from the field with the helicopter in it. Further away, but getting nearer, Adam could hear the sirens of police cars.

"Adam!" Phil Merchant called from the field. "Where have you been?"

Adam yelled at Phil, suggesting that he do something which was anatomically impossible. Last night, he'd been sure that Phil was the murderer. Two minutes ago, he was sure that it was Mark Rhodes. But he'd been wrong, both times.

Adam felt squashed, humiliated by his encounter with Naomi. Still, he hurried after her. There was a suspicion building in him as he ran, a suspicion that he'd got the whole thing horribly wrong from the start. He no longer cared what danger was involved. He was involved in this mess, and he needed to see it through. Tanya came running up to him.

"Adam, you're meant to be hiding!"

"Not now, Tanya."

"Did you see who was on the helicopter? It was . . ."

Adam walked faster to get away from Tanya. He supposed that Naomi really saw him the way he used to see Tanya – as an annoying pest who now and then came in useful. Ahead of him, Naomi reached the cottage door. She went inside. Adam pushed the door open. Mark Rhodes stood beside the kitchen table with a sad look in his eyes. His hands were empty. Naomi spoke impatiently.

"Where's the revolver, Mark? What have you done with it?"

Adam came and stood by her. A voice spoke from the next room.

"I've got it. It is mine, after all."

Adam recognised the man with the gun in his hand. Naomi turned to face him.

"Oh," she said. "It's you, Dad."

17

In the flesh, Paul Nelson looked older than on television. His face was wrinkled and his hair was thinning. But he was the first rock star Adam had seen close up, and his presence seemed to fill the room.

"*You're* Naomi's father?"

Nelson nodded. He put the revolver down on the table next to Mark Rhodes.

"You must be Adam. Mark's just been telling me about you and your father. Please, sit down."

Adam did as he was told. The rock singer turned to his daughter. Naomi stood, in her black sweatshirt and jeans, as still as a statue.

"Mark called me as soon as Kate died. He told me everything."

Naomi was staring at the floor. Nelson held out his hand and lifted her chin, until their eyes met.

"Why did you do it, Naomi?" he asked, softly. "Why did you kill Kate?"

Any doubts that Adam had left vanished as he saw the blank look on Naomi's face. When she spoke, all the mocking, mature quality had gone from her voice.

"I told her that Mark and I were in love. She told me I had to leave. She said that the school couldn't afford another scandal. Then she told Mark that he couldn't see me again."

The pieces fell into place for Adam. It wasn't Kate Dance who Mark Rhodes stayed behind to spend the summer with. It was Naomi. Nelson continued to question his daughter.

"And the others – why did you shoot them?"

Naomi seemed incredibly calm. *She's not normal*, Adam realised, still absorbing the shock. *Why didn't I notice before?* He'd been so bound up in the crush he had on her that he hadn't thought about the way she behaved. He hadn't considered that she might be a suspect, too.

Naomi spoke softly. Her voice betrayed no guilt about what she'd done.

"When Adam told me about the conversation he overheard in the woods, I realised that Forrest had guessed. I knew that Mo already suspected about me and Mark, so I decided to get them both. If Simon hadn't been there too, it would have been easy. I'd have made it look like Mo killed Forrest and then herself. But then I heard Simon, running away from the shots. I tried to shoot him, but he got knocked out. So I decided to make it look like he'd done it, instead."

Adam's mind started to jump ahead. He spoke to Naomi.

"When you came up to Lord Forrest and me in the woods yesterday, you were looking for the third bullet, weren't you?"

Naomi's voice took on an adolescent sneer.

"You were *so* blind. You didn't see me pocket that bullet, did you? You should have realised that I'd go straight to the police when you told me about Simon's affair with Kate. And you even reminded me about Mo. I went to the hospital twice, trying to get her alone so that I could finish her off."

Adam didn't react. Naomi couldn't hurt him any more. She couldn't make him feel any more stupid than he already felt. He was sorry for her. But there was one more thing he had to know.

"Those shots," he asked her, "a week ago, when Simon and I arrived – was that you, too?"

Naomi nodded.

"You kept thinking that Forrest fired at you," Naomi said, triumphantly, "even after I killed him. I shot at the car because I was trying to scare Simon off. I didn't want him in the cottage keeping me apart from Mark. Then you told me that Forrest was around that afternoon. So, before I killed Kate, I planted the shotgun in Forrest's room."

Naomi sat down. Adam was staggered. Forrest had been in the right, after all. He remembered the boy warning him about Naomi once: *you want to watch her*, he'd said. Forrest knew about her affair with Mark even then, and told Mo Highton that Naomi might have murdered Kate. That knowledge cost him his life.

"Didn't you suspect?" Adam asked Mark.

The English teacher shook his head.

"Kate spoke to me. She explained about Naomi's background and why I had to break up with her – Naomi might be nineteen, but the tabloids would still have had a field day: 'Rock Star's daughter gets sex education from her English teacher!' So I told Naomi that we had to finish, the morning before Kate died."

All this happened just before Naomi had taken him for a walk, Adam realised. She must have had the duplicate key cut while he was flicking through CDs in Hebden Bridge. Mark went on.

"But I never really suspected that Naomi was the one who shot Kate, and Mo, and Forrest. . . . If I had, I would have told the police about us. It was only when Naomi went to see Mo again this morning that I started to suspect. I rang the hospital, told them not to leave Naomi alone with Mo. Then, when everyone was out watching Paul's helicopter land, I decided to search. . . ."

His voice tailed off. He was on the verge of tears.

Paul Nelson was shaking his head, slowly.

"It's not your fault, Mark. I should have come over as soon as you phoned me about Kate's death, instead of finishing the tour first. They were my guns she used. She sneaked the revolvers and the shotgun out of my weapons cabinet over the summer. If anyone's to blame, it's me."

He turned to his daughter.

"The doctors told me you were better, Naomi. *You* told me you were. They'll never let you out this time. Do you understand that? Never."

"I don't care," Naomi said. "I don't care any more."

She pointed out of the window. Her voice had taken on a childish, sing-song quality.

"Here come the police. They'll take me away."

As everyone turned to look, Naomi reached forward and grabbed the gun.

"No!"

Paul Nelson shouted. Naomi lifted the gun. Adam wasn't sure who Naomi meant to shoot: him, her father, Mark or herself. He only knew that he was the one nearest to her. Time seemed to slow down to the speed of a slow-motion video replay. No-one could react fast enough. As Naomi's finger moved towards the trigger, Adam pushed the table away from him, banging it into her legs. Before she could react, he barged Naomi with his right shoulder, knocking her to the ground.

The gun went off.

The next moment, all hell broke loose. The kitchen door burst open. The room was filled with police officers. Adam saw Phil Merchant in the doorway, staring at him in disbelief. Mark Rhodes and Paul Nelson stood over him. They were both speaking, but Adam couldn't understand what they were saying. He watched as blood began to spread across his chest. It was as though he was there, but not there at the same time.

Then he blacked out.

18

"You know," Tanya said, as she closed the lid of the out-of-tune piano, "Forrest's dad paid for this teaching block. So they'll never build the TV studio here now."

"I wonder if it's insured," Matthew said. "You could burn it down, Tanya, and make it look like an accident. Then the school could use the insurance money to keep itself running."

While talking, he tapped on a cardboard box, keeping time with the twelve-bar blues that Adam was playing. Adam stopped and put the old Spanish guitar down. His shoulder ached where the bullet had grazed it the week before.

"According to Simon, the school's bankrupt," Adam told the others. "All the students who left after the shootings hadn't paid their fees."

"My IT teacher's resigned," Tanya said. "She just upped and left."

"She's not the only one," Adam told her. "Both the science teachers and the maths teacher have gone, too. There's only Mark, Simon, Geoff and Thérèse left. Oh, and Phil Merchant, of course."

"I could teach science," Matthew suggested. "I knew more than they did, anyway."

"How's Mo?" Tanya wanted to know.

Mo had come out of her coma four days ago, the day after Kate Dance's delayed funeral.

"They say she should make a full recovery by Christmas," Adam informed them. "Don't suppose any of us will be here to see her then."

He pulled a small loose-leaf notebook out of his jeans' back pocket and scribbled down a couple of lines for the song he was working on. When he'd finished writing, Tanya spoke again. "What'll you do next?" she asked Adam.

"My mum gets back from holiday tomorrow. I'll see if she can still offer me a job stacking supermarket shelves. What about you?"

Tanya made a grimace. "I'm too young to get a job. I'll have to go home and terrorise my parents. Maybe the council will give me a home tutor."

She propped up her chin with a fist.

"Do you know what qualifications you need to get into the Fire Brigade?"

They were still laughing when the door opened.

"Excuse us."

Simon was escorting Paul Nelson into the room. The singer was dressed in jeans and a leather bomber jacket.

155

He looked more like a car mechanic than a rock star.

"This was going to be the recording studio," Simon told him.

Nelson looked around the ramshackle room, with its bare floorboards and endless loose electrical wires.

"How's Naomi?" Adam asked.

"It'll be a long time before we know," Nelson told Adam. "The police don't think she'll ever go on trial, now that they know her history."

"What history?" Adam asked.

"I'm sorry," Nelson said. "I suppose I owe you all an explanation."

Nelson sat down by the piano, lit a cigarette and took a deep drag on it. "I was one of the first students at the Grange School. I began when I was thirteen. It was the late sixties – we didn't do much work, but I learnt to play guitar and had a lot of fun. I knew Kate then. She was one of the first batch of students, too. But she was a year older than me and took her education seriously, so we weren't close.

"In 1970, Nancy arrived, Kate's sister. She was a year younger than me, and we hit it off straight away. We were inseparable for two years. Then she got pregnant. Naomi was born on Nancy's sixteenth birthday, in October, 1972. I'd finished at the school by then. Kate had gone to Oxford. Nancy and I stayed with her parents while the baby was born. I didn't hang around for long afterwards. I was too young for parenthood, I guess. So was Nancy, but she had no choice in the matter.

"Anyway, I left. I spent the rest of the seventies playing in bands and sleeping on floors. I saw Nancy and

Naomi occasionally, but not enough to be a real dad to Naomi, or a real friend to her mother. I never sent money. I rarely had enough to feed myself. Nancy got depressed a lot, was hospitalised twice. There were drugs, too – they began to destroy her. That was when her parents threw her out. They tried to keep Naomi, said she wasn't safe. But Nancy wouldn't let them. I still blame myself for not being there for Naomi, then.

"Nancy and I lost touch. I was busy forming Call to Arms and starting to get successful. Once the band got its first gold disc, I did the usual rock star thing – bought an expensive house, big cars, got engaged to a model. On my wedding day, Nancy killed herself. My marriage was the final straw. She used an old army pistol of her father's. Naomi was nine at the time. She found her mother's body.

"I didn't find out about Nancy's death until I came back from honeymoon. I immediately went to see Naomi, but I couldn't get through to her. She didn't speak for several weeks. By the time she was ready to come out of psychiatric care, my marriage was over and I was wracked with guilt about what had happened. I insisted that she came to live with me.

"Of course, it was no life for a young girl. She had a nanny. I was touring nine months out of every year and recording the rest. I kept giving her money and presents, but she always resented that I hadn't been there for her mother. I wasn't really there for her, either, and she knew that, too. When she was thirteen, I tried sending her to various boarding schools. But it never worked out. Other girls hated her having a famous father whose poster was on their walls. Naomi used to pretend she was an orphan.

"I did try, believe me. I split up the band and spent as much time as I could with Naomi. I tried to get her interested in the music business, but she didn't want anything to do with it. She said she wanted to get an education, but every school she went to threw her out. The last one, when she was sixteen, she attacked another student with a pocket knife. For the next two years, she was in and out of institutions, seeing a lot of therapists, trying to start over.

"Kate suggested that Naomi came to Beechwood Grange as soon as she got the job here, two years ago. At the time, Naomi wasn't interested. But, after another year in an institution, the Grange School started to look a lot better to her. She'd gone on visits there with Nancy when she was a child. It must have had some happy memories for her.

"I wrote to Kate and she agreed to admit Naomi in January this year. Only Kate and Mo Highton knew about Naomi's background. Everyone else thought that she was coming to do 'A' levels late because of a long spell with glandular fever.

"Kate assured me that it was all a huge success. Kate got on with Naomi, was almost a second mother to her. Naomi wasn't really ready for 'A' levels, but she was bright and impressed her teachers, especially Mark Rhodes. When Naomi told me that she wanted to stay at school over the summer, I was delighted. So was Kate."

He sighed.

"The rest you know. Mark made up some story

about writing a novel in order to spend the summer with Naomi. I can't blame him too much. She was an attractive, intelligent teenager only four years younger than him. They were happy together, for a while. But Mark had no idea about her background and how unstable it made her."

Nelson stood up.

"So, Simon, what do you plan to do next?"

Simon scratched his chin.

"Enjoy my freedom, I suppose. Take a break. Get to know Adam a bit better, if he'll let me. I'll need to find a new job. Don't know what yet, with this recession set to last forever – anything but teaching."

"That'd be a waste," Nelson told him.

Simon shrugged disconsolately.

"I can't see any school having me after all this. I don't think I'd want to work in a state school again, anyway."

Paul Nelson leant forward earnestly.

"This school would have you."

Simon gave a wry smile.

"This school is bankrupt."

Paul Nelson shook his head.

"Not any more. I've arranged to pay off the school's debts. I've given the trust that runs the school enough to have the teachers' salaries paid, too."

Simon was taken by surprise.

"That's very impressive, but . . ."

"Listen," Nelson interrupted. "I've met with the school governors and with Mo Highton in the Airedale Hospital. They all support my plan."

"What plan is that?" Simon asked.

"I owe the Grange a lot," Nelson continued. "I can't

let it die because of what's happened this term. If you're willing to take it on, I'm willing to put more money in, so that you can make the place what Kate wanted it to be."

"What do you mean?" Simon asked. " 'Take it on'?"

Nelson spoke seriously.

"I'd like you to take Kate's place, to be the Headteacher."

Simon blinked twice.

"But you already have a Headteacher, Phil Merchant."

Nelson shook his head.

"Not any more. The governors asked Phil to resign this morning, when they got some information about his past."

Matthew, Tanya and Adam looked at each other. It was Tanya who spoke.

"What information?"

Nelson smiled.

"It's quite ironic, really. When the three shootings took place, Merchant treated the Press badly – refused to give out any information. That frustrated the reporters on the case, one of whom had had dealings with Merchant before."

"What do you mean," Adam asked, "dealings?"

Nelson explained.

"It seems that, two-and-a-half years ago, Merchant rang the *News of the World* and offered them a scoop – the full run-down on controversial goings on at Beechwood Grange School. His only condition was complete anonymity."

Adam was stabbed by anger at the Deputy Head's

deceit and hypocrisy. He remembered how Merchant had had a go at him after his encounter with the reporter.

"When the articles came out," Nelson went on, "they had the result that Merchant intended. The Head was forced to resign. But the effects were stronger than that. Several other teachers left and the school was in crisis. Merchant was made acting Headteacher for a term that year, as he has been this term. But the governors decided that they needed a new broom. Instead of giving Merchant the job permanently, they brought in Kate.

"The reporter Merchant had given the story to rang the Chair of Governors yesterday. He told her that, if they were thinking of appointing Phil Merchant to replace Kate Dance, there was something she ought to know. As a result, the governors agreed to sack Merchant yesterday afternoon." Nelson allowed himself a small smile. "I hear he didn't take it very well."

The smile turned into a grin.

"So, Merchant's gone and we urgently need a replacement. We need someone experienced – someone who shares Kate's ideals and philosophy – and, ideally, someone who can start tomorrow."

He looked at Simon.

"You have the confidence of the staff, and you've helped keep the school going this week, when you had every reason to get out of here. There'd be enough money for you to employ the new teachers the school needs, too. What do you think?"

Simon looked around the shabby room they were sitting in.

"I don't know what to say."

Nelson pleaded.

"Think about it, at least. Sleep on it."

"I don't need to sleep on it," Simon told him. "It all depends on one thing."

"Name your price," the rock star insisted. "I'll pay."

"It's not about money," Simon told him.

He turned to Adam.

"If I take the job, will you stay at the Grange? Will you give me, and it, another chance?"

Adam looked from his father to Naomi's father and back again.

"Yeah." He paused. "But I have a condition."

"What is it?"

Adam looked at Paul Nelson.

"You have to fund this place properly – finish building this studio for a start."

"Done," said Nelson.

Adam turned to his father.

"And I want to go and visit my mum tomorrow, make things up with her."

"No problem."

"Also," he smiled at Matthew and Tanya, "I need to pick up my guitar. I'm thinking about starting a new band."

Adam checked his watch and stood up.

"I've got to get a move on."

Simon looked confused.

"Why?"

"It's nearly three. I've got a tutorial to go to."

Adam pushed the door open. Without looking back, he stepped out into the autumn sunshine.

* * *

They were having an Indian summer. Several students were sunbathing on the grassy banks of the river. Adam was tempted to join them. He stood watching for a while, thinking about the father he hardly knew and the fresh life that they were about to begin together. Then he thought about Naomi, and how her life had been ruined before it ever really started. Finally, Adam thought about Kate Dance, and Forrest. The damage done to Naomi had destroyed their lives, too.

Then he turned away from the river and walked up the hill towards the Grange, his school.

Don't miss the next thrilling mystery in the new POINT CRIME series!

FORMULA FOR MURDER

The school field was still damp with dew as the Dearings security officer marched to the patch of land monitored by video camera E5. He expected to find a sad, bewildered old man with a straggling white beard, wearing a greasy raincoat and clutching a dubious bottle of alcohol. He wasn't prepared for the cold, lifeless body of a smartly dressed young man . . .

THRILLERS

R.L. Stine
- ☐ MC44236-8 The Baby-sitter $3.50
- ☐ MC44332-1 The Baby-sitter II $3.50
- ☐ MC46099-4 The Baby-sitter III $3.50
- ☐ MC45386-6 Beach House $3.25
- ☐ MC43278-8 Beach Party $3.50
- ☐ MC43125-0 Blind Date $3.50
- ☐ MC43279-6 The Boyfriend $3.50
- ☐ MC44333-X The Girlfriend $3.50
- ☐ MC45385-8 Hit and Run $3.25
- ☐ MC46100-1 The Hitchhiker $3.50
- ☐ MC43280-X The Snowman $3.50
- ☐ MC43139-0 Twisted $3.50

Caroline B. Cooney
- ☐ MC44316-X The Cheerleader $3.25
- ☐ MC41641-3 The Fire $3.25
- ☐ MC43806-9 The Fog $3.25
- ☐ MC45681-4 Freeze Tag $3.25
- ☐ MC45402-1 The Perfume $3.25
- ☐ MC44884-6 The Return of the Vampire $2.95
- ☐ MC41640-5 The Snow $3.25
- ☐ MC45682-2 The Vampire's Promise $3.50

Diane Hoh
- ☐ MC44330-5 The Accident $3.25
- ☐ MC45401-3 The Fever $3.25
- ☐ MC43050-5 Funhouse $3.25
- ☐ MC44904-4 The Invitation $3.50
- ☐ MC45640-7 The Train $3.25

Sinclair Smith
- ☐ MC45063-8 The Waitress $2.95

Christopher Pike
- ☐ MC43014-9 Slumber Party $3.50
- ☐ MC44256-2 Weekend $3.50

A. Bates
- ☐ MC45829-9 The Dead Game $3.25
- ☐ MC43291-5 Final Exam $3.25
- ☐ MC44582-0 Mother's Helper $3.50
- ☐ MC44238-4 Party Line $3.25

D.E. Athkins
- ☐ MC45246-0 Mirror, Mirror $3.25
- ☐ MC45349-1 The Ripper $3.25
- ☐ MC44941-9 Sister Dearest $2.95

Carol Ellis
- ☐ MC46411-6 Camp Fear $3.25
- ☐ MC44768-8 My Secret Admirer $3.25
- ☐ MC46044-7 The Stepdaughter $3.25
- ☐ MC44916-8 The Window $2.95

Richie Tankersley Cusick
- ☐ MC43115-3 April Fools $3.25
- ☐ MC43203-6 The Lifeguard $3.25
- ☐ MC43114-5 Teacher's Pet $3.25
- ☐ MC44235-X Trick or Treat $3.25

Lael Littke
- ☐ MC44237-6 Prom Dress $3.25

Edited by T. Pines
- ☐ MC45256-8 Thirteen $3.50

Available wherever you buy books, or use this order form.

Scholastic Inc., P.O. Box 7502, 2931 East McCarty Street, Jefferson City, MO 65102

Please send me the books I have checked above. I am enclosing $_____ (please add $2.00 to cover shipping and handling). Send check or money order — no cash or C.O.D.s please.

Name _____ Birthdate _____

Address _____

City _____ State/Zip _____

Please allow four to six weeks for delivery. Offer good in the U.S. only. Sorry, mail orders are not available to residents of Canada. Prices subject to change.

point®

Other books you will enjoy, about real kids like you!

☐ MZ42599-4	**The Adventures of Ulysses** Bernard Evslin	$3.25
☐ MZ43469-1	**Arly** Robert Newton Peck	$2.95
☐ MZ45722-5	**Dealing with Dragons** Patricia C. Wrede	$3.25
☐ MZ44494-8	**Enter Three Witches** Kate Gilmore	$2.95
☐ MZ40943-3	**Fallen Angels** Walter Dean Myers	$3.95
☐ MZ40847-X	**First a Dream** Maureen Daly	$3.25
☐ MZ44479-4	**Flight #116 Is Down** Caroline B. Cooney	$3.25
☐ MZ43020-3	**Handsome as Anything** Merrill Joan Gerber	$2.95
☐ MZ43999-5	**Just a Summer Romance** Ann M. Martin	$2.95
☐ MZ44629-0	**Last Dance** Caroline B. Cooney	$3.25
☐ MZ44628-2	**Life Without Friends** Ellen Emerson White	$3.25
☐ MZ42769-5	**Losing Joe's Place** Gordon Korman	$3.25
☐ MZ43419-5	**Pocket Change** Kathryn Jensen	$2.95
☐ MZ43821-2	**A Royal Pain** Ellen Conford	$2.95
☐ MZ45721-7	**Searching For Dragons** Patricia C. Wrede	$3.25
☐ MZ44429-8	**A Semester in the Life of a Garbage Bag** Gordon Korman	$3.25
☐ MZ47157-0	**A Solitary Blue** Cynthia Voigt	$3.95
☐ MZ43638-4	**Up Country** Alden R. Carter	$2.95

**Watch for new titles coming soon!
Available wherever you buy books, or use this order form.**

Scholastic Inc., P.O. Box 7502, 2931 E. McCarty Street, Jefferson City, MO 65102

Please send me the books I have checked above. I am enclosing $ _____
Please add $2.00 to cover shipping and handling. Send check or money order - no cash or C.O.D's please.

Name _____ Birthday _____

Address _____

City _____ State/Zip _____

Please allow four to six weeks for delivery. Offer good in U.S.A. only. Sorry, mail orders are not available to residents of Canada. Prices subject to changes.

PNT89